SUDAN
The Lion of Truth

[The Angel and the Lion]

Lee McQueen

2nd Edition

McQueen♟Press
Des Moines, Iowa

Published by McQueen Press
info@mcqueenpress.com
http://www.mcqueenpress.com

About the Author
Lee McQueen's roots stretch deep into the world of writing, research, analysis, and public affairs. She writes short stories, poems, novels, and screenplays.

1st Edition "The Angel and the Lion" screenplay registered with the Library of Congress as "The Angel and the Lion," alternative title "SUDAN: The Lion of Truth." 1st Edition "The Angel and the Lion" screenplay registered with the Writers Guild of America, west, as "SUDAN."

"The Angel and the Lion" short story first published in 2006 in *Imaginarium*.

On cover, "Darica Lion 07174." Nevit Dilman. Wikipedia Commons. 2007. Interior design and typesetting by Lee McQueen.

Logo registered mark of McQueen Press.

© 2011 Lee McQueen

Publisher's Cataloging-in-Publication
McQueen, Lee
SUDAN: The Lion of Truth / Lee McQueen
p. cm.
ISBN 978-0-9798515-9-9

1. Slavery—Sudan—Fiction 2. Christianity and politics—United States 3. United States—Foreign Relations 4. Adventure fiction 5. Conspiracies—Fiction 6. Dallas (Tex.)—Fiction 7. Khartoum (Sudan)—Fiction 8. Atbarah (Sudan)—Fiction 9. Motion picture plays. I. Title

Works by Lee McQueen

Short Story Collection

Imaginarium

Poetry

Things I Forgot to Tell You

Novel

Kenzi

Celara Sun

Screenplay

Kindred

Non-Fiction

Writer in the Library!

It's not where you're from.
It's where you're going...

Everything you've ever learned saves your life.

For Mom

Table of Contents

Introduction

"While on a Christian mission to redeem slaves in Sudan, a reformed female gang member is kidnapped and sold into slavery herself."

"Harriet Tubman meets Foxy Brown meets Ellen Ripley."

"Action/adventure set in Dallas, Khartoum, Atbarah, and Kassala."

"An ex-female gang member from South Dallas, Davey, joins a Christian mission to redeem slaves in the Sudan. Through a betrayal from one of the mission members, she is sold into slavery herself. She uses her former street experiences and talent for leadership to convince the other slaves to break free and flee to the Ethiopian border."

"While the locations sound extremely exotic and probably expensive, half of the film takes place in South Dallas. Also, sections of the Texas-Mexico border region would substitute for Sudan. In addition, work as extras might prove beneficial to displaced Katrina survivors in the Dallas and Houston area."

I used the above statements to pitch and query *The Angel and the Lion* to Stan Lathan & Russell Simmons at Simmons Lathan Media Group, F. Gary Gray, O'Shea "Ice Cube" Jackson at The Firm Beverly Hills, John Singleton, Carl Franklin at William Morris Agency, Laurence Fishburne at Paradigm, Wesley Snipes at Amen-Ra, Spike Lee at Forty Acres and a Mule, Will Smith at Overbrook, Nona Gaye at Innovative Artists, James Cameron at Light Storm Entertainment, Oprah Winfrey at Harpo, BET Movies, Dallas Film Commission,

Austin Film Festival, American Screenwriting Competition, in addition to various agents.

Austin Film Festival let me know that my screenplay would not advance to the next round. I received the only other reply from Nona Gaye's agent at Innovative Artists expressing conditional interest (I admitted to them that I had no production budget). Unfortunately, I didn't receive a reply from any of the producers on the list. But I believed and still believe in the script and the story. So now it's published by McQueen Press with the all the accessories. Someday, maybe on a long flight or car trip, one of the above players that I admire so much might read *The Angel and the Lion* and decide to take it on. Maybe.

In the meantime, I completed *Kindred*, the screenplay adaptation of the book by Octavia Butler. I completed *Kenzi*, the novel. I completed *Things I Forgot to Tell You*, the poetry collection. I completed *Imaginarium*, the short story collection. I feel very good about the short story collection because I wrote all fourteen short stories for easy conversion to screenplay format. My family history and two more short story collections are the next writing projects on my growing list. But for now, the focus is *The Angel and the Lion*. Enjoy!

Lee McQueen
22 October 2006

Update:

Since the publication of the first edition of *The Angel and the Lion*, McQueen Press released its first novel *Kenzi* and the second edition of *Things I Forgot to Tell You* in 2007, the first non-fiction reference *Writer in the Library!* in 2008 (still very popular), and the second novel *Celara Sun* in 2010.

While the first edition of *The Angel and the Lion* was 8 ½ x 11, the second edition has been adjusted to traditional trade paperback size, 6 x 9 for easier distribution. Besides the new cover, while there have been additions and deletions to the front and back matter and minor punctuation edits to the short story, the text of the actual screenplay remains unchanged.

I leave it to producers, directors, cinematographers, and others to determine the always necessary adjustments for translation to the silver screen.

Lee McQueen
July 31, 2011

"Darica Lion 07168." Nevit Dilmen. Wikipedia Commons. 2007.

SUDAN: The Lion of Truth

The Angel and the Lion
Short Story

Davey came to in a dimly lit, moving space that rattled over the sound of a loud motor. Lifting her aching head gingerly, she saw that she wasn't alone. She was with the other women–fourteen all together. All of them were black.

She was American with shoulder-length braids. They were southern Sudanese with scarves and head wraps. The red surge of pain inside her skull receded to a dull throb which allowed her small intervals to remember the betrayal.

Congressman Bradley, warned her three weeks ago.

"Davey, don't go. I know you feel that you owe Minister Thompson for helping you when you were incarcerated, but negotiating large sums of money with individuals who have already shown a degree of immorality by buying and selling humans, is too high a price to pay. You don't owe him or the United Church of Peace Mission your life."

"Congressman, you are the father I never had and I love you for that. But I want to make peace with the world. I've done a lot of taking and a lot of hurting. At least I can say that I tried. It's just for three weeks."

"Davina Lewis..."

"Minister Thompson has faith in me, Congressman. I wish that you did."

They compromised. Davey accepted a text messenger and promised to send Congressman Bradley daily updates from Sudan.

She'd come a long way from the streets of South Dallas and the gangster life she'd led most of her younger years on the liquor and convenience store circuit. During her two-year prison sentence, she met Minister Thompson who helped her to study for her G.E.D. Once paroled, she worked for his organization, The United Church of Peace Mission.

One day, Congressman Bradley strode into the mission and laughingly asked her to cease sending all those letters to his office about the Sudan slave trade—Minister Thompson's crusade. After she completed her parole, Congressman Bradley invited her to work in his office because, "Despite all those trees you killed, the letters were well-done."

And now, despite Congressman Bradley's warning, despite preparation and Christian goodwill, Davey, twenty-five and rehabilitated, hung from a chain attached to shackles on her wrists that twisted around a bar in the back of the truck. She watched miles of Sudan desert and the occasional tamarisk tree rush away in clouds of sand and dust through the back opening with growing despair.

The United Church of Peace Mission's effort to redeem slaves in Sudan was not only a dismal failure. It was a slaughter.

They arrived to Khartoum that morning and met their guide, Salim, on the tarmac.

"You are exactly on time. Welcome to Sudan. Did you have a good flight?"

Minister Thompson briskly took charge.

"Great flight! We're ready to go to work. Are we all set to meet them?"

"It has been arranged."

And now they all knew what it was that had been arranged. After a pleasant tour of Khartoum, Salim drove them a few miles north where the slavers held thirteen captives. The mission participants, college students and middle-class retirees, looked at the slaves they came to redeem in the back of the truck. While the others went to negotiate up front, Davey lingered.

"How long have you been here?"

The slaves stared back at her silently. The entire scenario seemed so unbelievably obscene... and wrong. Congressman Bradley told them Western dollars only fueled the trade by driving up the price. He'd told them.

Davey swallowed.

"We're doing what we can to free you."

Still no response.

Davey peeked around the truck and watched money exchange hands. She pulled out the text messenger:

YES 13 SLVS

Chaos erupted loudly in front of the truck. A quick glance revealed screams of fear, streaks of blood, and twitching bodies in blazing afternoon heat. Quickly, she sent another message:

ATTK SOS

No place to hide. Under the truck? In the back of the truck? Run for the desert? It happened too quickly. The slavers grabbed her. She struggled. They hit her. And now, like her own ancestors, she was a slave.

"Where are we going? Where are they taking us?"

No answer. She could speak neither Dinka nor Arabic. Davey had never felt so alone. Not even during her week in solitary for beating another inmate near to death. She lost the text messenger. No one knew where she was or where she was going. She didn't even know. Davey rocked back and forth as the truck rattled over endless desert terrain.

A few hours later, the slavers opened the truck and pulled them all roughly to the ground.

"Atbarah," she heard one of the slaves whisper to another.

When the slavers traded them again and led them to another truck, Davey noticed the headlights of a car in the darkness. After another half hour of rough terrain, they led the captives into a warehouse with a main room and a few smaller rooms.

The men threw food on the hard floor and poured water into a bucket. Davey drank water from her hands.

She heard a voice shouting Arabic roughly and turned to see one of the slavers waving his gun. The women around her sat and faced the wall. Davey quickly did the same. From behind, she heard the sounds of a struggle.

"Davey, are you okay? We're going to get out of here."

Minister Thompson must have been held in the car.

"Davey, don't fight them. Do as they say!"

Davey heard angry, rapidly-spoken Arabic reprimanding him. She half-turned and then quickly faced the wall again. Sure enough, she heard the meaty sound of a gun butt striking her mentor in the gut as he was led away.

One by one, they dragged the women into a smaller room. The screaming started and stopped as the women returned. Even if Congressman Bradley received her text message, he would not be in time. Davey heard the by now familiar Arabic command followed by a smack of the gun butt directed at the young Dinka girl beside her.

She looked about ten-years-old.

Davey thought of those days long ago on the streets of Dallas. Talking loud but saying nothing really as the cop snapped the cuffs on her and told her she needed to do something with her life. There was more to the world than the streets she and her friends thought they controlled. There was also more to friendship than mutual self-destruction. She received not a single visit or letter from her crew during her two years inside.

The little girl cried.

Davey looked down in shame at her own powerlessness. She felt prickles of fear.

She was next in line.

She told Minister Thompson on his first visit that she only agreed to see him to break up the boredom of her day. He told her about Shadrach, Meshach, and Abedneggo.

"I Been a Negro, too," was her sarcastic response.

Minister Thompson laughed and told her that was funny. he had to laugh with him. She could never rattle him and eventually, she stopped trying. He'd persuaded her to read the story of Daniel in the lion's den aloud.

With a quick prayer to God to deliver her from the lions too, Davey stood up slowly, still facing the wall. The inevitable angry shouts and curses rained down upon her. She felt the gun butt strike her in her back but spoke calmly.

"Take me instead."

The girl gasped. Outrage ensued. The slaver dug the gun barrel crunchily against her spine.

"English? Or American?"

Davey winced.

"American."

With that, they grabbed her braids and dragged her into another of the smaller rooms. Minister Thompson sat opposite the desk of the leader in some sort of macabre interview.

The slaver holding her hair spoke rapid Arabic. She heard the word "American" tossed out indignantly as he shook her. The man behind the desk smiled with polite mockery as he spoke in British-accented English.

"I am Asaad el Haak. The Lion of Truth. Welcome. Please remain standing as there are only two chairs and we are still in deep discussion."

El Haak turned back to Minister Thompson in thoughtful contemplation.

"The Great America. The new land for the children of the old lands. Were you born an American, Minister Thompson?"

"Yes."

"Where in America were you born?"

"El Paso."

"How about you, Miss..."

"Dallas."

He didn't need to know her name.

"Two Texans!" El Haak was delighted. "The cowboy and his cowgirl from the Wild West. JR Ewing. The land of oil and greed." He paused. "Texas was a slave state prior to America's own Civil War. With great fields of cotton picked by, I believe it was... slaves. Am I right, Minister Thompson."

"That's true, for a brief period."

"Would it not be a most intriguing irony to learn that your ancestor's once owned Miss Dallas' ancestors? And now you are here to make amends by teaching Miss Dallas how to set slaves free."

Minister Thompson remained silent. The baiting continued.

"You must feel very at home in the Middle East, Minister Thompson. It is not so different. Do you like it here? You are here. Therefore, you must surely like it here."

Davey's head ached from the fist in her hair and the sound of El Haak's hateful, mocking voice.

"You have already experienced so much of the joy and pain there is to find here in the desert -your unfortunate pain, my everlasting joy. There is not much else to know."

El Haak waited. She and Minister Thompson waited.

The interview disappointed El Haak. She could tell, though he smiled, that their passivity puzzled and irritated him. She felt El Haak's hard, black gaze travel up and down her body and then shift back to Minister Thompson as if making up his mind.

That type of cruelty, she'd seen once before. In a tiny apartment in a South Dallas slum, her father questioned her mother... and then strangled her as Davey watched from underneath a table.

El Haak's gaze focused on Minister Thompson with finality. Davey's eyes filled with tears as she looked at El Haak pleadingly.

Davey heard Minister Thompson's voice from far away.

"Don't cry, Davey."

El Haak glanced back at Davey and smiled, finally satisfied. From behind the desk, he withdrew a sword with a metallic hiss.

What good did crying ever do anyone?

Asaad El Haak lifted his sword and cut off Minister Thompson's head amid Davey's screams of protest. Davey's knees weakened as his skull thumped to the floor.

The fist in her braids snapped her back upright to meet El Haak's smiling contemplation as her tears mingled with Minister Thompson's blood.

"Minister Thompson will always be part of Sudan," he informed her conversationally.

He held the sword against her neck... and waited.

Davey closed her eyes and tried to still her shaking body as the blade scraped up and down slowly, softly. Her breath choked in and out.

"I think you will too, Miss *Davey* of Dallas. My assistants appear extremely eager to introduce you to our special ways."

The slaver holding her led her to where she sat before. She heard El Haak shout something and two slavers guarding the other women went into his office and carried out both parts of Minister Thompson's body.

Davey shivered violently. The women who had been to the small room and the women yet to go had all been completely cowed by the sound of Davey's screaming.

Davey looked down to avoid the hard gaze of the remaining slaver as he approached her. Something acrid bubbled in the back of her throat. He hit her with the gun butt.

If Davey understood Arabic, she would have heard, "Get up filthy black American slut! *We* are your god now!" She understood enough to stand. She followed him in a trance.

The slaver watched her undress slowly. If she cooperated, maybe she wouldn't be hurt. She was down to her underwear. She unhooked her bra.

But was she willing to die?

He put down his gun. He reached down and pulled himself out of his pants.

Yes.

Davey kicked him hard and cut off his scream with a hard blow to the throat. She forgave her father as she strangled the slaver. He had no further need of his gun, knife, or radio. She took them. Dressed quickly. Peeking out of the room, she saw that the other women remained unguarded. *Mother, I was too young and too small to help you.* Davey swallowed.

"Ssss."

They all turned to her. She passed all except the gun to the first woman who had been raped.

The other two slavers, finished with Minister Thompson, were on their way back inside—probably to take their turn with her judging by the laughter.

Davey positioned herself and brained the first slaver who entered. Three of the women dragged down the other slaver before he could raise his gun. While Davey snatched their guns and radios away, the women quietly, viciously took their revenge with the knives.

Now, three of them had guns.

Davey felt a glimmer of hope. They might have a chance.

"Who speaks English?" she whispered. The women shook their heads. "English!" she demanded desperately.

The little girl who sat next to her earlier spoke up.

"I speak English."

"You!" Davey was exasperated, "Then why..."

The girl was contrite. "I was afraid."

Understandable.

Davey decided rapidly. "Tell them we're gonna take a truck!"

The girl translated for the women and they all nodded, agreed. The slavers, mutilated and bloodied, said nothing.

El Haak raised the alarm from his office doorway. Davey aimed and fired. Missed.

No turning back.

She could hear other slavers responding to El Haak's shouts. They outnumbered the women.

Davey screamed, "Fight for your lives! Fight them!" She shot down two henchmen as they ran into the room.

"Get the guns!"

The odds turned. Caught unaware because they didn't expect the women to fight back, five more henchmen fell screaming and cursing, twitching.

Nine women gunned with her.

"Stay with me!" she told the girl.

They ran into the night for the same truck in which they'd arrived, shouting and shooting at everything and everyone who moved to stop them.

Davey took weapons detail in the passenger seat. The universe brought her full circle to her first after-school job.

The woman behind the wheel announced to Davey, via the girl, "We head for Gondor through Kassala!" The other women continued shooting out of the back of the truck as they fishtailed wildly away from the warehouse.

Good-bye, Minister Thompson.

"I'll contact Congressman Bradley from Ethiopia. He'll help us." Davey replied.

If the Lion of Truth followed, she would pray to God to give her the strength to close his mouth and destroy him.

Perhaps a sandstorm would hide them.

For now, at least, they were safe.

The Angel and the Lion
Screenplay Synopsis

ACT I

   SUDAN opens at a museum in Khartoum with SALIM, a mysterious, chameleonic "go-to" guy being ordered by his employer to infiltrate a powerful group of slavers led by ASAAD EL HAAK (The Lion of Truth). SALIM'S EMPLOYER wants slave trading to end so Sudan can raise itself from an economic, political, social, and cultural morass.

   At the same time, DAVEY (Davina Lewis), a young African-American woman, begins her new crime-free life after being paroled from the Dallas prison system for armed robbery. Davey struggles to readjust to mainstream society and to sever ties with GIGI who tries to pull Davey back to the streets. Davey is assisted by MINISTER THOMPSON for whom she does community service. BROTHER DENNIS helps Davey obtain a GED. AUNT HELEN, the brother of Davey's dead father, helps Davey to understand she must forgive herself and others for past mistakes. CONGRESSMAN JARED BRADLEY offers Davey a receptionist position in his office. Congressman Bradley's nephew, JACE BRADLEY, is the police officer who ran Davey off the streets and put her in prison years ago. He is attracted to Davey now and speaks to her about the future.

   Minister Thompson contacts Congressman Bradley to agitate for action on the slave trade in Sudan. Davey joins Minister Thompson's trip to redeem slaves in Sudan. With his employer's blessing, Salim establishes a side deal with Brother

Dennis to allow the mission to be taken for ransom just north of Khartoum. Salim and his employer wish to provoke the United States to shut down Asaad el Haak. Brother Dennis just wants a slice of the ransom and possibly to get rid of Minister Thompson. Unknown to Salim, Brother Dennis cuts another deal with the kidnappers to sacrifice a few members of the mission.

ACT II

Congressman Bradley and Aunt Helen initiate individual efforts to find out what happened to Davey. Salim's employer is a powerful figure in the political and economic spheres of both the U.S. and Sudan. He is also an acquaintance of Congressman Bradley and so instructs Salim to reveal the bare outline of what has happened to Congressman Bradley, but not the entire story. Congressman Bradley is unable to generate publicity or permission for a rescue so he calls his nephew, Jace (now no longer a cop) for assistance. Aunt Helen joins Congressman Bradley and Jace to plan the rescue.

While Congressman Bradley, Jace, and Aunt Helen raise money, Minister Thompson and Davey are transported to a warehouse in Atbarah, Asaad el Haak's headquarters. Davey decides to keep a low profile and pass as Sudanese. When the slavers attempt to rape a young girl, Davey reveals herself as American. Asaad el Haak verbally torments Davey and Minister Thompson. At the same time, Jace interrogates Brother Dennis. Asaad el Haak kills Minister Thompson. Just as a slaver prepares to rape Davey, her street life attitude surfaces to assist her escape and that of the other Sudanese women and one boy (who speaks English). The women acquire a truck and a highway chase/shoot-out begins. Davey uses the boy as a translator and directs the women to fight their way towards the Ethiopian border so they can find help in Gondor. A sandstorm forces a halt. The women hide the truck in the garage of an abandoned building to wait out the storm.

Jace flies to Gondor and crosses the border in a humvee to locate Davey. The slavers figure out the location of the women and drive towards the building. Davey tells the women to stand and fight. The firepower of the slavers overwhelms the women. They escape through a tunnel under the building that leads into the desert near Jace. After several deaths, Jace, Davey, and the remaining women escape in another truck abandoning the humvee. After Jace and Davey stop to fix a flat, the slavers catch up and another shoot-out ends with Asaad el Haak blowing himself up in Jace's hot-wired humvee. Jace and Davey and the women cross the Ethiopian border protected by human rights organizations and European media.

ACT III

Back in Dallas, Davey confronts Brother Dennis. At the same time, Congressman Bradley is offered the chance to avenge himself on Davey who is connected with the death of his brother, Jace's father. Instead, Congressman Bradley exhausts favors and decides to sacrifice his congressional office to buy protection for Jace, Davey, and Aunt Helen from investigatory fall-out regarding the disappearance (death) of Brother Dennis and possible charges of terrorism and conspiracy. As his swan song of defiance, Congressman Bradley writes a book about the entire episode blowing the whistle to the international public on the lukewarm response by various North American organizations on the issue of the Sudan slave trade. Brother Dennis's murderer reveals himself in the credits.

The Angel and the Lion

Screenplay

Written by

Lee McQueen

FADE IN

EXT:DAY:SUDAN:NATURAL HISTORY MUSEUM

Two men stand together, their backs turned, facing the
museum. SALIM smokes. SALIM'S EMPLOYER doesn't.

> SALIM'S EMPLOYER
> We were once great. We will be
> again.

> SALIM
> Does it have to be all or nothing
> at all?

> SALIM'S EMPLOYER
> Can two come together without
> becoming one?

> SALIM
> Should they?

> SALIM'S EMPLOYER
> Brown father. Black mother. And
> we are the children. The trade
> will have to end, Salim. To do
> that, you must become one of
> them.

> SALIM
> Lies for truth.

> SALIM'S EMPLOYER
> You have friends in the West.

SALIM
If they are friends (pause), then
they are welcome.

Credits.

EXT:DAY:DALLAS:LEWIS HOUSE:FRONT PORCH:

Davey, 27, leaves HELEN LEWIS'S house eating a
banana.

DAVEY
Bye, Auntie Helen. See you
tonight.

Before she can walk away, Helen undoes the two prison-
style French braids Davey still wears and fluffs her hair.

HELEN
I want you have a good first day
at work. You look beautiful.

Helen hugs Davey. Then Davey walks down the sidewalk.

INT:DAY:DALLAS:RESTAURANT:KITCHEN

Davey and her SUPERVISOR look at a mountain of dirty
dishes piled into the sink.

SUPERVISOR
When you're finished, check with
me. I'll show you where we keep
the brooms and mops.

EXT:DAY:DALLAS:STREET

At noon, Davey walks towards the mission. GIGI yells to her.

> GIGI
> Day-VEE! What up, girl? I heard they cut you loose.

Gigi and Davey hug.

> DAVEY
> What up, Gigi? You know I had to raise up outta there. That is not the place to be and I ain't hardly goin' back. I'm handling my business now.

> GIGI
> Handling business? Why you ain't called your girl to roll wit chu?

> DAVEY
> You wanna wash dishes too?

> GIGI
> You work there?

> DAVEY
> Yeah, I just started.

> GIGI
> Oh what? You want fries wit dat? Naw we ain't got no mayonnaise, whitey. Aw shit! Nobody gonna believe this!

DAVEY
See that's all right though.

GIGI
Girl, fuck *this*. Lemme tell you
what the real is. Stop by my house
tonight. We doin' a thing. Get you
back on your feet with the
quickness instead of picking food
up off the floor and wrapping it
up.

DAVEY
Okay, Vir-gin-ia.

Gigi mock flexes at Davey.

GIGI
Oh, watch it now!

DAVEY
We don't do that.

Davey mock flexes back at Gigi.

DAVEY
At least I don't.

Davey and Gigi laugh.

DAVEY
But naw though. I'm gonna keep
my head low and work my way
through it all. You know?

GIGI

I'm just saying though. You know
where to find me. Everytime we
did a hit, we did it for you. We
always said, "To Davey!" at the
end of the night. You true blue.

DAVEY

I looked for you to check me out
while I was inside.

Long pause.

GIGI

I know girl. I just couldn't make
it, you know? I got warrants and
shit happenin'. All that metal and
concrete. Not for the kid. You was
on my mind though. True blue.
And you hung tough. Running
shit. Respect. Get at me tonight.
We gonna be back on top the way
we used to be.

DAVEY (looks distracted)

I'll holla. I gotta get to my other
job though.

GIGI

Uh oh! She work hard for the
money.

Davey and Gigi hug.

EXT:DAY:DALLAS:STREET:OUTSIDE MISSION

Jace, 32, casual dress, leans against a patrol car. He holds a stop-watch.

>   JACE
> Right on time.

Davey looks at him in recognition and contempt.

>   DAVEY
> Don't you have somebody else's
> rights to violate today?

Davey uses her middle finger to stroke her hair back.

>   JACE
> I got the day off. That's cute, by
> the way.

Davey turns to enter the mission.

>   JACE
> Davina.

>   DAVEY
> Cop.

>   JACE
> I just wanted to see how you were
> doing.

>   DAVEY
> Obviously, I'm doin' my parole.
> Damn, they just give anybody a
> gun these days.

>   JACE
> How's it going?

DAVEY
I ain't gotta tell you nothin'.

JACE
No, you don't. But you can listen
a minute. Davina, I'd rather not
see you back inside. Not again. I
didn't want to bring you there the
first time. But it had to be you.
You were the leader.

DAVEY
You don't care about nothing but
that badge and that gun.

JACE
Davina-

DAVEY
I ain't feelin' protected and
served, man. Do your damn job!

Jace laughs.

DAVEY
I cannot stand you.

JACE
You don't need to tell me you
can't stand me, Davina. I can see
the hate in your eyes.

Their raised voices mingle.

DAVEY
My name is Davey, punk
motherfucker!

JACE

And my name is Officer Bradley,
Davey!

Davey shakes her head with impatience.

DAVEY

Who are you? My fuckin' father?
This ain't no Oprah Show.
Nobody asked you what the fuck
you think about me.

JACE

No, I'm not your father, Davey. I
would never do what your father
did.

Davey remains silent, turns her back on him, and crosses
her arms.

JACE

Davey, you hurt people. Most of
all, you hurt yourself. Now you
have a chance to make things
better.

Jace takes a step closer to Davey.

JACE

If I see you - and I *will* see you,
Davey. If you go back to your old
ways (pause) I'll bust you again.
And it won't be nice. (takes
another step closer) It won't be so
easy. Do you hear me, Davey? Get
it together while you still have a
chance.

DAVEY
I see the hate in *your* eyes.

Davey stares at him a moment then enters the mission.

INT:DAY:DALLAS:MISSION

MIN. THOMPSON
Davey, welcome.

DAVEY
Thank you. Thank you for the
opportunity to work here and for
speaking up for me.

MIN. THOMPSON
You are definitely not ordinary,
Davey.

DAVEY (fighting tears)
In four years, you and Brother
Dennis and my auntie were the
only ones who visited. And that
cop. (pause) Everyone else just
had excuses.

MIN. THOMPSON
Davey, you have no idea the
places you'll go and the things
that you can do.

DAVEY
The things I did and the places I
went got me locked up.

MIN. THOMPSON
You have a big effect. You change
the lives of everyone you meet in
extraordinary ways. It's a talent.

DAVEY
It's a curse.

MIN. THOMPSON
A gift – when used properly. But
we've already spoken of this. Let
me show you around and tell you
what we do here. That's your
desk.

DAVEY
My desk, serious? I never really
had a desk before.

MINSITER THOMPSON
That's your very own desk. Have
a seat and try it out. You can put
your purse in the bottom drawer
and hang your sweater here.

Davey sits and folds her hands looking very pleased.

MIN. THOMPSON
As you know, this is a Christian
mission. We are witnesses for
God for all who wish to know
Him better. We are in the church,
the streets, and the prisons. It
doesn't matter. Wherever we are
led, we go. Are you aware of the
slave trade in the Sudan?

Davey shakes her head.

MIN. THOMPSON
This is a map of Sudan. They have
been fighting a civil war for over
twenty years. Armed militia
called muraheleen from the
Baggara tribes raid civilian Dinka
populations for women and
children. Most of the raids take
place here, in Bahr El Ghazal.
They are held captive and forced
to work for free in western Sudan.
They are often physically and
sexually abused. It is a terrible
evil.

DAVEY
I didn't know there was still
slavery.

EXT:DAY:SUDAN:VILLAGE

Huts in a Sudanese village are aflame. Animals lay
slaughtered. Children cry in the background.

INT:DAY:SUDAN:VILLAGE:HUT

There is blood spattered on the wall.

Two shouting and laughing soldiers (#1 & #2) wrestle a
screaming Dinka woman to the ground.

SOLDIER #3 enters the hut and sees the rape about to
take place.

Soldier #3 speaks quietly in Arabic.

                    SOLDIER #3
            Mine. Only mine. Always mine.

Soldier #1 & #2 curse him in Arabic.

Soldier #3 raises his gun and shoots Soldier #1 between
the eyes.

The woman screams in fear.

Soldier #3 points his gun toward Soldier #2 who freezes.

                    SOLDIER #3
            The Lion waits for you.

Soldier #2 exits the hut quickly.

Soldier #3 removes his sunglasses and stares at the
woman who cowers and stares back at him.

Soldier #3 is Salim.

INT:DAY:DALLAS:MISSION

Davey sits with DENNIS.

Dennis is thirtyish, clean cut, with glasses.

                    DAVEY
            The settlers wanted freedom from
            the oppressive Mexican
            government.

                    DENNIS
            No.

                    DAVEY
            But the book says-

DENNIS
Mexico threatened their
economic wherewithal. (leaning
in closer) People will steal, kill,
and cheat to protect their money.
Don't be fooled by hidden
agendas. But when it comes time
to take the GED (shrug) go by
what the book says.

Davey stares at Dennis with a blank expression.

EXT:DAY:SUDAN/KENYA BORDER

A truck rumbles along the road then stops next to a
waiting van.

Salim exchanges money with a man.

Salim unchains the Dinka woman from the back of the
truck and firmly pushes her towards the man.

SALIM
Kenya.

The Dinka woman tries to thank him.

Salim interrupts her coldly and points his gun.

SALIM
Walk away. If you come back, I
will kill you.

The woman stumbles back from Salim.

INT:DAY:DALLAS:MISSION

Davey types letters and makes copies of articles and book chapters.

She answers the phone and sends faxes.

She makes coffee. She sits in meetings.

INT:DAY:DALLAS:JARED'S OFFICE:PRIVATE OFFICE

Jace stops in for a visit as Jared tries to shove the drawer filled with Davey's letters closed.

>   JACE
> Hey, Unc! What are you doing?

>   JARED
> Trying to figure out a good place
> to bury all these trees the United
> Christian Something Mission
> killed.

>   JACE
> You mean the United Church of
> Peace Christian Mission?

>   JARED
> You know those people?

>   JACE
> I know someone who works
> there. She's probably the one
> typing all that up for you.

JARED
They want me to do something
about the slave trade in Sudan.
We got enough problems right
here in South Dallas. There's not
a whole lot I can do, actually.
Sudan is a sovereign nation. But,
then again, everybody wants a
piece of me these days. I bet
you're glad you're not a cop
anymore.

JACE
Those streets don't love me.

INT:DAY:DALLAS:MISSION

MIN. THOMPSON sits with Davey.

Davey rolls her eyes as Min. Thompson pulls out some
books.

DAVEY
You really like doing this?

MIN. THOMPSON
I like to discuss the Word of God.

DAVEY
We both know I'm only doing this
with you because it'll look good to
my parole officer.

MIN. THOMPSON
The Word of God has a way of
healing the spirits of many in
many different ways.

DAVEY
As long as ole dude gets off my
tip.

MIN. THOMPSON
Remember what we talked about
last time?

DAVEY
Them three boys.

MIN. THOMPSON
In the third chapter of the Book
of Daniel. Do you remember their
names?

DAVEY
Yeah, I remember. Shadrach,
Meshach, and I Been a Negro.

MIN. THOMPSON
Abednego.

DAVEY
Those names are too long.

MIN. THOMPSON
How do you feel about
Nebuchadnezzar? Can you say it
really fast?

Davey laughs.

                    DAVEY
        No.

                    MIN. THOMPSON
        Do you remember what happened
        to Shadrach, Meshach, and... I
        Been a Negro? That actually is
        kind of funny.

They laugh together.

                    DAVEY
        They went into the fire but the
        fire didn't burn them.

                    MIN. THOMPSON
        And do you know why?

                    DAVEY
        Because they were faithful and
        wouldn't bow to a false god.

Davey looks up with a suspicious expression.

                    DAVEY
        You trying to tell me something
        about getting locked up?

                    MIN. THOMPSON
        Well, there was this man named
        Daniel who had a pretty close
        encounter with some lions-

INT:DAY:DALLAS:MISSION

A few months later, Jared visits United Church of Peace
Christian Mission. Davey sits at her desk.

                    JARED
I would bet you're an excellent
typist.

                    DAVEY
I do okay.

                    JARED
More than okay. I'd say, an
undiscovered virtuoso of the
keyboard.

                    DAVEY
You think I don't know what
virtuoso means.

                    JARED
Well, of course you know what it
means, Miss-

                    DAVEY
    Lewis.

Davey is amused and waits to see what he'll say next.

                    JARED
I see the coffee's made over there.
The fax machine and copy
machine's humming. Pencils and
pens at the ready. Where would
this office be without Miss Lewis,
Undiscovered Virtuoso of the
Keyboard?

Jared points to Davey's printer.

                    JARED
Why, there's a letter in the printer
now! I interrupted you.

Davey shrugs.

> DAVEY
> Naw. I do that everyday.

> JARED
> Everyday?

Jared leans over her desk to read an envelope.

> JARED
> URGENT. Well since it's *urgent*,
> why don't I cut out the middle
> man and save you a stamp?

Davey understands who he is and shakes her head.

> DAVEY
> Nice to meet you, Congressman
> Bradley.

> JARED
> Likewise, Miss Lewis.

> DAVEY
> Your son never mentioned you.

> JARED
> My son?

> DAVEY
> Officer Bradley?

> JARED
> My *nephew*, *Mister* Bradley, likes
> to maintain his own identity. You
> know how this younger
> generation is.

DAVEY
Oh. Nephew. My bad. Did you
say Mister?

JARED
Oh he didn't tell you?

DAVEY
Well, we don't exactly talk.

Jared looks at her speculatively.

JARED
Uh *hunh*. As of a month ago, Mr.
Bradley is a private citizen.
Nowadays, I think he prefers to
catch people before trouble
happens instead of after.

DAVEY
He told you about me?

JARED
He didn't tell me you were an
Undiscovered Virtuoso of the
Keyboard. I had to come here to
find that out for myself. Which is
why you were undiscovered. But
not anymore. Miss Lewis, please
tell Min. Thompson that these
letters are no longer necessary. I
will call him this week.

EXT:DAY:DOWNTOWN DALLAS:BUS DEPOT

Davey waits for a bus. She wears t-shirt, jeans, and
tennis shoes with her hair pulled back into a ponytail.

                    PRISON COMMITTEE
                    (voice)
          -solve your problems through
          violent measures rather than
          reason and logic. Based on this,
          it's quite obvious to everyone in
          this room, including yourself,
          that you have serious anger
          issues. Do you have anything at
          all to say for yourself?

Davey looks at several sophisticated women talking on
cell phones, swinging briefcases, wearing expensive
clothes, shoes, and sunglasses.

                    DAVEY
                    (voice)
          No.

One such sophisticated woman walks out of an office
building and waits.

Davey and the woman make eye contact but don't say
anything.

                    PRISON COMMITTEE
                    (voice)
          You mess up again, Miss Lewis,
          and you're right back where you
          started. *Only more so.* If they tell
          you to jump, you better get on a
          pogo stick and put your back into
          it.

A sports car pulls up to the curb in front of the woman. It
is Jace.

                    PRISON COMMITTEE
                    (voice)
Well? Are you gonna sit in a hole
and be angry or are you gonna
learn about Jesus and turn the
other cheek?

Davey takes a quick glance down at herself. Jace jumps
out to open the woman's car door.

                    DAVEY
                    (voice)
Learn about Jesus.

Davey walks away and looks into a store window. Jace
catches a glimpse of the back of Davey's head.

EXT:DAY:DALLAS:ZOO

Davey happily strolls through the Dallas Zoo from cage
to cage eating an ice cream cone and runs into...

Gigi and OTHER MEMBERS OF HER OLD GANG who
talk loudly and horse around.

                    GIGI
Got the day off, hunh?

                    DAVEY
Can't work all the time.

                    GIGI
But you do. Davey got two jobs
y'all. You shoulda told me you
was coming to the zoo. I woulda
picked you up.

DAVEY

Naw, I don't like to ask around
for favors too much. People
would get tired of seeing me
coming and go the other
direction.

GIGI

Seem like you the one goin' the
other direction though. Every
time we see you, you on your way
to somewhere else.

DAVEY

I ain't in that life no more, Gigi.
For real.

GIGI

Girl-

DAVEY

It ain't nothin' nice to be told
when to eat and where to shit and
for how long to do both.

GIGI

You changed. White man got you
scared, hunh?

DAVEY

Scared? Please, Gigi. I'm the one
that stepped to it and did a bid.
Me! (voice raising) Where the
fuck were you? (lowers voice) I'm
saying, I did what I did. All that
shit. I did it. That was *me*. I'm
tired of goin' nowhere with that.
So now I'm doing something else.

> GIGI
> (looking away)
> You just ain't down no more.

> DAVEY
> You're right. I don't get down like
> I used to. We had our time-

> GIGI
> Let's go ya'll.

Davey overhears mutters and the word, "sellout."

> PRISON COMMITTEE
> (voice)
> We don't want to see you. We
> don't want to hear you. We don't
> want to smell you. We don't want
> to know you. We're sick of you
> and so are the taxpayers of Texas.

Gigi looks back at Davey. Davey meets her gaze steadily.
Then Gigi leads the gang away.

INT:EARLY EVENING:DALLAS:MISSION

> MINSTER THOMPSON
> To Davey, everyone!

Echoing shouts of "To Davey!"

Davey picks up the rest of her things from her desk in a
cardboard box. Min. Thompson hugs Davey.

> MIN. THOMPSON
> I'm gonna miss you, Davey.

                    DENNIS
        I'll walk you home.

                    DAVEY
        You don't have to. It's still light
        out.

                    DENNIS
        I wanted to talk to you.

EXT:DUSK:DALLAS:MISSION

Davey and Dennis walk. Dennis carries Davey's box of
belongings.

                    DAVEY
        You didn't say much inside.

                    DENNIS
        I keep things to myself
        sometimes. You've come a long
        way since we first met.

                    DAVEY
        Well, I hope so since we first met
        while I was locked up.

                    DENNIS
        Another lifetime. And now you
        don't have to ever worry about
        that again.

                    DAVEY
        I'm not worried. My life is back
        on course. I'm gonna start in the
        Congressman's office next week.

DENNIS
No more burgers and fries?

DAVEY
I'm ready to take it up another
notch.

DENNIS
Yeah. Me too.

DAVEY
You too?

DENNIS
I've got pretty ambitious plans.

DAVEY
Like?

DENNIS
Like, asking you out. Davey, I've
been wanting to get to know you
better all this time. But, I didn't
want to make things complicated.

DAVEY
Complicated like my parole?

DENNIS
Well, I wasn't going to mention it.

DAVEY
Look, Brother Dennis-

DENNIS
Just Dennis, please.

                    DAVEY
          Dennis. I'm trying to bring focus
          back to my life. Things were just
          raggedy and strung out all over
          the place. I've got some lost time
          to make up for. Helping Auntie
          Helen and doing my job are what
          I'm about now. I'm sorry. You
          understand though, right?

                    DENNIS
          Yeah. I feel you. But when you're
          ready, and when the time is right,
          don't forget about me. First dibs,
          okay?

EXT:NIGHT:LEWIS HOUSE:FRONT PORCH

Davey takes back her box of belongings.

                    DAVEY
          Let's just see what happens.

INT:NIGHT:LEWIS HOUSE:SITTING ROOM

Helen jumps away from the front door and picks up a
department store catalog. Davey enters.

                    HELEN
          Well, how did your last day go?

                    DAVEY
          They threw me a party.

HELEN
Was that one of them that walked
you home?

Davey sits down with a mocking glance.

DAVEY
Oh you saw that.

HELEN
Oh well I was passing by the
window reading my newspaper.

DAVEY
Your newspaper or this phone
book?

HELEN
Oh now Davey! So, you excited
about working for Congressman
Bradley?

DAVEY
Very. I can finally do some things
I've always wanted to. Help you
pay off this mortgage.

HELEN
Oh now you just worry 'bout you.
The congressman's been in office
a long time now. That'll be a
good, steady job. You done well
for yourself, Davey. (sighs) You
look so different than when you
first came. You was kind of
tentative. Real nervous, all
twitchy-like. Edgy. But you got
your confidence back.

DAVEY
Yeah. I feel almost normal.

HELEN
Oh come on, now. What's
normal?

Helen makes a crazy face and they laugh together.

HELEN
Davey. We can't change the clock
back. I can't take back what my
brother did. But if I'd known how
bad things were, and... if I'd been
a different kind of person, I
would have come got you long
ago.

DAVEY
Auntie Helen, don't. Please. I
don't blame anyone. Not
anymore. I'm here now. So are
you. Things are okay.

HELEN
Look. I ain't cho mama. Least not
directly. God rest Marian's
blessed soul. So I can't really tell
you how to be and where to go
and how to do.

DAVEY
Okaaaay.

> HELEN
> You don't have to rush on love. I
> know sometime we women thank
> jus 'cause some man have a nice
> job or talk nice or act nice, we
> have to get all breathless. It's
> okay to wait for the real one to
> come along. And he will. Maybe
> not today or tomorrow, or even
> next year. But he'll be along.

> DAVEY
> I know, Auntie. I promise you I
> won't rush into anything. I know
> how to play it cool.

> HELEN
> (stern)
> Just remember you just as good
> as anybody out there, Davey. Sure
> you had some problems and did
> some things as people do
> sometimes. But you made up for
> your mistakes. You don't have to
> stand at the back of the line for
> anyone or take any less than what
> life has for you.

Davey begins to cry.

> HELEN
> You a good person, Davey. Trust,
> Auntie. Auntie ain't gonna lie to
> you. You leave the rest and wait
> for the best. Hear?

Davey nods. She and Helen hug.

HELEN
I changed my mind. You ain't just
as good as everybody else. You
better. Set your alarm and get to
the Congressman's office early.
You be there first. You go to the
front of the line. Not the back.

Davey laughs.

INT:DAY:DALLAS:JARED'S OFFICE:RECEPTION
AREA

Davey wears a suit, muted makeup, and her hair is worn
in microbraids, then gathered into a bun.

DAVEY
So nice to see you as always.

JACE
Well, I do write the songs that
make the whole world sing.

DAVEY
As long as you don't.

JACE
Let's get married.

Jace hands her a bouquet of flowers. Davey looks at him
like he's crazy.

JACE
Gotcha! I didn't know if my uncle
would remember with a raise, but
I did. Congratulations on your
first six months of keeping him
out of trouble for me.

>   DAVEY
> I can't even believe you
> remember stuff like this. But
> thank you.

Davey gives him a grudging smile and takes the flowers. Jace stands and looks at her.

>   JACE
> Oh my God, she smiled! I didn't
> think that was allowed. Who said
> you could do that? That didn't
> hurt you did it? Are you okay?

>   DAVEY
> He's expecting you.

Jace enters Jared's private office as Davey smells the flowers and smiles wider.

INT:DAY:JARED'S OFFICE:PRIVATE OFFICE

>   JARED
> Well, well, well. I wish I could say
> this is an unexpected surprise,
> but you've been buzzing around a
> lot lately since a certain young
> lady joined my staff.

>   JACE
> I got nothin' but love for you,
> Unc!

>   JARED
> You got a wide-open nose is what
> you got. How are things at South
> Oakcliff?

JACE

I'm making a difference, I think.
Martial arts class is going good.
I'm still saving up for my own
studio.

JARED

That same young lady wouldn't
happen to have anything to do
with your career change?

JACE

Man, you still on that? Naw. I
figure, we're given one chance at
one life. And I'm taking all that
that one chance and that one life
have to offer me. Couple of years
from now I should be ready to
make my move.

JARED

On the studio or my receptionist?

Jace laughs, embarrassed.

INT/EXT:DAY:DALLAS:JACE'S SPORTS CAR

DAVEY

I don't know why we're doing
this. I already know how to drive.

JACE

Yeah, I know. I just like to keep
the streets safe.

DAVEY

You ain't a cop no more.

                    JACE
No. ut as you can plainly see,
(strokes dashboard) I do have a
nice ride. I don't want you out
there driving all wild in your
hoopty and then scratching it up
trying to parallel park.

                    DAVEY
You probably like this car more
than your girlfriend.

                    JACE
What girlfriend?

Davey is silent.

                    JACE
Aah! avey, Davey, Davey. hat
was you I saw that one time
downtown.

                    DAVEY
I was shopping.

                    JACE
So you thought that was my
girlfriend.

Davey shrugs.

                    DAVEY
Who cares?

                    JACE
Right. ho cares? ot Davey. Davey
don't care. Davey don't care about
nothin'!

                    DAVEY
          Hel-lo, Jace? Aren't you supposed
          to be teaching me how to drive?

Davey presses the accelerator, then brakes hard. Davey
and Jace jerk back and forth.

                    JACE
          Give me the damn keys.

Jace and Davey switch sides.

                    JACE
          We're through for today.

                    DAVEY
          You were getting off topic.

                    JACE
          Anyway. I want to show you
          something.

EXT:DAY:DALLAS:EMPTY STOREFRONT

Jace and Davey sit in the car and looks at it.

                    JACE
          Almost there.

                    DAVEY
          Almost where?

                    JACE
          There.

                    DAVEY
          What's there?

JACE
My studio.

Davey looks incredulous and scornful.

DAVEY
You trying to be a rapper?

JACE
Martial arts. A few years from
now if I stay focused.

Davey gives Jace a significant look.

DAVEY
And on topic.

Jace and Davey look through the glass storefront.

DAVEY
What will you call it?

JACE
Oh, I don't know. Jace's Chop
Socky & Soul Food Shop.

DAVEY
You are never serious.

JACE
I'm seriously starved. hat are we
standing here for? et's get
something to eat.

INT:DAY:DALLAS:JARED'S OFFICE:RECEPTION
AREA

Davey answers the phone.

                    DAVEY
          Doing just great.
          Nebuchadnezzar!

                    MIN. THOMPSON
                    (voice)
          Nebuchadnezzar to you too! See,
          there's nothing you can't do,
          Davey! I always believed that.

                    DAVEY
          I know. Hold on a second.
          Congressman Bradley's expecting
          your call.

Davey presses an intercom button.

                    JARED
          Yes?

                    DAVEY
          Min. Thompson on line one.

INT:DAY:DALLAS:JARED'S OFFICE:PRIVATE
OFFICE:

                    JARED
          There are certain vested interests
          not willing to take a strong stand
          on the issue. It always dies in
          committee. I tried to light some
          fires, but there's always someone
          with a bucket of water standing
          close by.

MIN. THOMPSON
Well, then it's a good thing that
Plan B is ready to go.

JARED
Plan B. Am I going to like Plan B
any better than Plan A?

MIN. THOMPSON
Exactly one month from now,
we're going to Sudan to redeem
as many slaves as we can. Mostly
college students and retirees.
They're using their own financial
resources for travel. People
believe in this work,
Congressman, even if our
government doesn't.

JARED
That's a risky endeavor, Min.
Thompson. Many human rights
groups denounce the practice of
foreign redemption because of
fraud. Plus, foreign money drives
up prices to where native families
can't afford to buy back their
relatives. The Sudan government
will push for peace. Remember
the treaty?

MIN. THOMPSON
I understand the larger policy considerations, Congressman. But I'm also mindful of the welfare of the individuals waiting for the red tape to quit gumming up the works. People languish in chains while there's meeting after meeting and resolution after resolution.

JARED
Would this be your first trip to Sudan?

MIN. THOMPSON
The first of many.

JARED
Are you at all concerned about negotiating large sums of money in a foreign land (pause) with individuals who have already shown a degree of immorality by buying and selling humans?

MIN. THOMPSON
We've considered that. Someone from the university will brief us on the area. And Brother Dennis put us in contact with a guide and translator.

> JARED
>
> Davey, don't go. I know they
> helped you in the past, but you
> don't owe them your life.

> DAVEY
>
> Yes, I do. I do. You know that I'm
> going.

Jared looks as if he wants to argue further, but shakes his head in surrender.

> DAVEY
>
> Min. Thompson has faith in me. I
> wish that you did.

Jared hold's Davey's chin, looks into her eyes, and whispers.

> JARED
>
> I have more faith in you than you
> could ever begin to know, Davey.
> More than you could ever begin
> to understand. I always have.
> Even from that first day.

There is a sort of sexual undercurrent that startles Davey and makes her uncomfortable.

Davey breaks eye contact.

Jared is momentarily embarrassed and then brusque.

                    JARED
Well, I had to try to talk you out
of it. I actually bought some, ah,
we'll call them going-way
presents.

                    DAVEY
A beeper? And a barrette.

                    JARED
Not quite. This barrette holds a
GPS device. Global Positioning
System. You should braid it tight
to your hair. I can monitor you
from my computer. This is a text
messenger that will allow you to
send me updates. It also has GPS.

                    DAVEY
                    (laughing)
Oooh, they're so shiny!

INT:DAY:DALLAS:MISSION

The map of Sudan is on the wall behind the PROFESSOR
briefing the mission.

                    PROFESSOR
Sudan is culturally and religiously
diverse. Arabs populations
dominate the north. Various
African tribal populations
dominate the south. For
centuries, southern Sudan has
served as a lucrative source of
gold, slaves, and ivory for
northern Arab merchants and
traders.

Davey takes notes.

> PROFESSOR
> It was once a country of great
> ancient cities. Today, the civil war
> has left many resources in Sudan
> drained, destroyed, or yet
> undiscovered.

EXT:DAY:DALLAS:LOVE FIELD

The mission boards a plane from the tarmac. Helen
waves good-bye to Davey.

> PROFESSOR
> (voice)
> Sudan is one of Africa's hottest
> countries. It is 30% desert. Wind
> blows from the north continually,
> creating sandstorms known as
> *haboobs*.

INT/EXT:DAY:AIRPLANE

The mission looks out the windows to an overhead view
of the Nile River at Khartoum.

                    PROFESSOR
                    (voice)
          The Nile, with its tributaries,
          creates its own climate for
          agriculture along the banks and
          towards the southern part of
          Sudan which is another source
          for conflict. Due to war, drought,
          and famine, Sudan is currently
          one of Africa's poorest nations.

EXT:DAY:KHARTOUM:AIRPORT

The Mission, composed of Min. Thompson, Davey, five
COLLEGE STUDENTS, and two RETIRED COUPLES
arrives to the tarmac.

                    MIN. THOMPSON
          There's our truck. And that's our
          guide, Salim. Let's go everyone!

The group gathers its luggage and walks towards Salim.

                    DAVEY
          What made you decide to come to
          Sudan?

                    COLLEGE STUDENT
          I've been working with the
          mission for a year. Doing what
          you used to do, I think.

                    DAVEY
                    (laughing)
          Yes, we've been getting the
          letters. And they are excellent by
          the way.

COLLEGE STUDENT
I've been doing research for
several years. But I didn't want to
be one of those people who just
talks and writes about something.
I wanted to know first-hand.

DAVEY
I can respect that.

COLLEGE STUDENT
What about yourself? Why are
you here?

Davey doesn't have time to answer. They reach their
guide, SALIM.

SALIM
You are right on time. Welcome
to Sudan. Did you have a good
flight?

MIN. THOMPSON
Great flight. We're ready to go to
work. Are we all set to meet at
Khartoum?

SALIM
It has been arranged.

Salim is attracted to Davey.

He looks Davey over without her noticing.

INT/EXT:DAY:KHARTOUM:MISSION'S TRUCK:

SALIM
You can see there is an English
influence on the Arab style of the
layout here. You can also see the
shantytowns built by refugees
from the South.

MIN. THOMPSON
Those mosques look centuries-
old.

SALIM
Many of them are. North of
Khartoum, on the east bank of
the Nile, the ancient civilization
of Meroe thrived starting 400 BC
and it lasted 800 years. Meroe
had its own written language that
had nothing to do with Egyptian
hieroglyphics. Many people don't
know that. All you hear about is
Egypt's King Tut.

COLLEGE STUDENT
Look at that tamarisk tree. They
exude a sweet substance, sort of
like honey, called manna. Many
people believe it is this manna
that was eaten by the Israelites
when they fled Egypt.

The mission looks out the window at a river.

Davey takes pictures.

Salim glances at Davey in the rear view mirror.

                    SALIM
          This is the White Nile.

                    MIN. THOMPSON
          How many languages do you
          speak?

                    SALIM
          Many. English, of course. Arabic,
          French, Italian, Spanish, several
          African languages. But in Sudan,
          at least in the north, Arabic is the
          primary language. There is still
          resistance to Arabic from the
          south.

                    MIN. THOMPSON
          That sounds like the big debate in
          the States over including Spanish
          as an official language. And in
          Canada, there is a lot of conflict
          over the use of French in Quebec
          and other parts.

                    SALIM
          I don't believe it is quite the
          same.

Salim glances at Davey in the rear view mirror again.

This time she notices.

She glances away.

EXT:DAY:JUST NORTH OF KHARTOUM:MEETING
PLACE:

The guide parks next to another truck and car.

> SALIM
> That is the person to whom you
> would speak. The slaves are in the
> back.

The mission group walks to the back of the slaver's truck
and views the slaves. Everyone but Davey moves to the
front of the truck to observe the negotiation.

> SLAVE NEGOTIATOR
> Greetings.

Rapid Arabic is spoken between the Truck Driver and
SLAVE NEGOTIATOR. Min. Thompson looks a little
puzzled. A few men stand around with lowered weapons.

Davey looks at the hopeless and frightened slaves.

> DAVEY
> How long have you been here?

No response. She counts them. Eighteen women and two
children.

> DAVEY
> We're doing what we can to free
> you.

Davey peeks around the side of the truck and sees money
change hands.

INT:DAY:NORTH OF KHARTOUM:MISSION'S TRUCK

>   DAVEY
>   YES 18 SLVS

Davey looks up. One slaver packs away the money.

It seems everyone is just looking at each other.

Davey sees Min. Thompson ask a question. There is no answer. The missionaries look at each other.

The slavers open fire on the missionaries.

Davey ducks below the dashboard.

Davey sends another message amid gunshots and screams.

>   DAVEY
>   ATTK SOS

Still below the dashboard, Davey holds her camera up and takes several pictures.

Davey sees the keys are still in the ignition and reaches to pull herself up by the steering wheel.

Davey is yanked out of the truck while stuffing the camera into her bra while her back is to the henchmen.

EXT:DAY:NORTH OF KHARTOUM:MEETING PLACE:

Davey drops the text messaging device.

A slaver slaps Davey across the face then steps on the text messenger.

The bodies of the missionaries are robbed then buried in shallow graves.

Davey shudders and looks away.

Davey is led to the back of the slave truck.

She struggles. She is knocked unconscious.

Davey is chained, still unconscious, with the other slaves.

Salim appears upset but conceals it.

Min. Thompson is held separately in the car.

INT:DAY:DALLAS:SOUTH OAKCLIFF:GYMNASIUM

Jace finishes an afterschool martial arts class.

> JACE
> Next week, we're gonna pick up
> where we left off. Don't forget to
> practice your moves.

He towels off as his CLASSY FEMALE COMPANION walks up to him smiling.

> CLASSY FEMALE
> COMPANION
> Don't forget to practice *your*
> moves.

> JACE
> Show me some new ones tonight.

INT:DUSK:DALLAS:JARED'S OFFICE:PRIVATE
OFFICE

Jared checks Davey's GPS signals against the itinerary
she gave him.

He looks uneasy when he sees she's moving northeast.

INT:DUSK:DALLAS:LEWIS HOUSE:KITCHEN

Helen looks at the phone then the clock, then the phone
with worry.

Helen calls Dennis.

> DENNIS
> I haven't heard from them. It may
> be that they're just behind
> schedule. I'm sure she'll call soon.

Helen holds the phone looking very unhappy.

INT:NIGHT:DALLAS:JARED'S OFFICE:PRIVATE
OFFICE

Jared calls Dennis.

> DENNIS
> Yes, her aunt just called here. I
> haven't heard back from anyone
> yet either.

> JARED
> Call my office if you hear
> anything.

Jared dials a number.

                    JARED
          I need to you to check on
          something.

Two hours later Jared receives a phone call.

                  ANONYMOUS
                 (French voice)
          I am told of some thugs who
          high-jacked a truckload of
          missionaries from the U.S. The
          truck was stripped down to the
          frame a few miles away.

                    JARED
          Any survivors?

                  ANONYMOUS
          Unknown.

                    JARED
          What about the contact, Salim?

                  ANONYMOUS
          There is no such person.

                    JARED
          What do you mean?

                  ANONYMOUS
          A ghost.

                    JARED
          I see. Anything else?

                    ANONYMOUS
          That's all I can give you without
          compromising my own
          operations.

                    JARED
          Thank you.

The anonymous voice belongs to Salim.

                    SALIM
          Good luck, Congressman.

INT:DAY:SUDAN:SLAVER'S TRUCK

Davey awakens. She tries to communicate with FELLOW
CAPTIVES. No one can understand English.

                    DAVEY
          Where are we going? Where?

They answer her in Dinka and Arabic.

INT:DAY:DALLAS POLICE STATION

Helen pleads for assistance from an OFFICER at the
front desk.

                    OFFICER
          We don't handle international
          concerns such as this. Contact
          the embassy.

                    HELEN
          The embassy is closed!

OFFICER
Give it a few days and try again.

INT:DAY:DALLAS:NAACP OFFICE

Helen pleads for assistance from various organizations.

NAACP
Our focus is on the black
community here at home. We
cannot expend resources to do
rescue missions for persons who
voluntarily leave the country and
interfere with other nations.

INT:DAY:DALLAS:NOI MOSQUE

NOI
Many of the so-called Christian
groups that "redeem" slaves are
fronts for right wing political
groups. They actively inter with
and destabilize the sovereignty of
a nation involved with its own
internal conflicts. You'll never see
them speak out against the
military-industrial complex in the
U.S. which operates its own
domestic slave system supported
by prison labor.

INT:DAY:DALLAS:BAPTIST CHURCH PEW

        BLACK CHURCH
We will pray for Davey, Sister
Lewis.

INT:DAY:DALLAS:JARED'S OFFICE:PRIVATE OFFICE

Jared listens to an OFFICIAL from the United
International States, a political governing body, on the
telephone.

        OFFICIAL
        (voice)
      We have established a
      tribunal to investigate the
      matter of exploitation of
      women and children in the
      Sudan slave trade. As for
      the individual in question,
      there is nothing we can do
      at this point because of the
      treaty.

Jared listens to the SPOKESPERSON from World
Peace and Human Rights Today.

        SPOKESPERSON
        (voice)
     The situation you described to us
     is only one reason why we do not
     support the concept of slave
     redemption by foreign interests.
     But you know this, Congressman.
     We do recommend that you
     contact the UN to voice your
     concerns.

INT:NIGHT:DARK ROAD:SLAVER'S TRUCK

Davey rocks back and forth as she did in solitary.

She knows she is a slave.

She cries.

EXT:DAY:ATBARAH:ROAD

Food is thrown on the ground. Water is poured in a community bucket.

Davey doesn't eat, but she drinks.

The captives trade hands.

INT:DAY:ATBARAH:WAREHOUSE:SLAVE ROOM

> HENCHMAN #1
> (in Arabic)
> Silence! All of you Dinka camels
> and donkeys lower your eyes and
> face the wall!

Davey doesn't understand Arabic. She watches to see what the other women do and then does the same.

Min. Thompson is led through the room by HENCHMEN #2 & #3.

> MIN. THOMPSON
> Davey, are you okay? We're going
> to get out of here. Don't fight
> them. Do as they say.

                    HENCHMAN #2
                    (in Arabic)
          Who are you talking to? You are
          not allowed to talk. Silence you
          fat American pig!

Henchman #3 strikes Min. Thompson in the gut with the
butt of his gun.

Min. Thompson is led to one of the smaller rooms.

Davey recalls reading aloud to Min. Thompson while in
jail.

                    DAVEY
                    (voice)
          ...they brought Daniel, and threw
          him into the lion's den.

                    HENCHMAN #1
                    (in Arabic)
          Bitch! Get up! Now! Move!

Henchman #1 hits a woman in the back with the butt of
his gun. Henchman #2 returns and stands guard.

Screams of the woman come from the adjoining room.

Davey cringes and shudders. The screaming stops in the
pause during which the two henchmen trade off.

INT:DAY:ATBARAH:WAREHOUSE:EL HAAK'S ROOM

                    MIN. THOMPSON
          We're not here to cause problems.
          We're here to help those who
          need help.

ASAAD EL HAAK
I don't need your help.

MIN. THOMPSON
Slavery is not something that is
new. Many governments
sanctioned it. Slavery has been
practiced since the days of the
Bible. But it is now seen as a
practice that is no longer
necessary or welcome.

ASAAD EL HAAK
I guess that would depend upon
whether you ask the master or the
slave.

INT:DAY:ATBARAH:WAREHOUSE:SLAVE ROOM

Henchman #1 returns the raped woman and throws her
to the floor. The woman sobs.

Henchman #1 picks a young GIRL. Her MOTHER, the
sobbing woman, shrieks in horror and tries to grab for
her child. Henchman #2 beats her off.

HENCHMAN #1
(in Arabic)
Get up, little Dinka bitch!

DAVEY
(voice)
My God, sent his angel and he
shut the mouths of the lions.
They have not hurt me...

Davey inhales and exhales then stands up.

>   DAVEY
> No.

Henchmen #1&2 speak rapid Arabic and curse Davey.

>   DAVEY
> Me instead.

The words "American" and "English" are thrown around amid rapidly spoken Arabic. The henchmen argue.

The Mother hugs her daughter.

>   HENCHMAN #1
> British or American?

>   DAVEY
> American.

The two henchmen spit on the ground in contempt. Henchman #1 grabs Davey by her braids and drags her to el Haak.

INT:DAY:ATBARAH:WAREHOUSE:EL HAAK'S ROOM

Still holding Davey by her hair. In Arabic...

>   HENCHMAN #1
> She is an American.

>   ASAAD EL HAAK
> How did we acquire an American
> slave?

>   HENCHMAN #1
> They didn't tell us.

EXT:DAY:ATBARAH:WAREHOUSE

Salim's face is half-shadowed by sunlight as he services a truck.

INT:DAY:ATBARAH:WAREHOUSE:EL HAAK'S ROOM

The men speak more rapid Arabic.

Min. Thompson and Davey stare at each other.

Asaad El Haak looks Davey up and down and deliberately speaks English.

>ASAAD EL HAAK
>I am not yet sure.

INT:DAY:DALLAS:MISSION

Dennis writes on a notepad.

>DENNIS
>No, I'm sorry Ms. Lewis. I still
>haven't heard anything. I
>promise. I will definitely call you
>when I hear something.

INT:DAY:DALLAS:JARED'S OFFICE:PRIVATE OFFICE

Jared speaks on the phone.

BIG BUSINESS
It is a delicate time, Bradley.
Sudan is cooperates with the U.S.
on other issues. There is oil and
other minerals and resources in
the South that we need. Tobacco,
coffee, and tea interests have
been looking at various areas for
their own use when the fighting
stops. No one wants to aggravate
one side or the other. These
lobbies are pretty powerful as you
well know.

JARED
People are dying over there. One
of my own staff is out there. I'm
not gonna ignore this.

BIG BUSINESS
Don't make promises you can't
keep, Bradley. If you push the
wrong button, there's no telling
what you'll set off.

JARED
What are you really saying?

BIG BUSINESS
I'm saying (pause), keep several
things in mind.

INT:NIGHT:DALLAS:JACE'S LIVING ROOM:

Jace receives a call.

                    JACE
          I'll be there in fifteen minutes.

                    CLASSY FEMALE
                    COMPANION
          Jace, we have plans. I don't
          appreciate-

                    JACE
          Don't forget your purse.

EXT:NIGHT:DALLAS:JARED'S OFFICE

Jace's tires scream.

INT:NIGHT:DALLAS:JARED'S OFFICE: RECEPTION
AREA:

Jace enters. Then Helen enters tiredly, unseen.

                    JARED
          ...about six hours ago. I had the
          attack verified by another source.

Jared and Jace look at Davey's GPS signal at Atbarah.

                    JARED
          No one will negotiate her release.
          No one will go after her. (sighs)
          She's out there, Jace.

INT:NIGHT:DALLAS:JARED'S OFFICE:PRIVATE
OFFICE

Helen cries out from the doorway and they turn around.

                    HELEN
I knew it! She said that she would
call me when she got there. She
hasn't called. And no one knows
anything!

                    JARED
Someone always knows
something.

                    HELEN
They won't do anything. Not a
one of them.

                    JACE
I've got my passport. And some
weapons.

Jared shakes his head.

                    JARED
Jason-

                    JACE
She needs our help. You just said
there's no one else. Besides, I owe
her.

                    JARED
You love her.

Jace glances at Helen but doesn't respond.

                    JARED
How could you not. What will you
need?

JACE
No questions asked or answered.
And more weapons.

JARED
That means you need money. A
lot. I can get started on
arrangements tonight and have
you in the air tomorrow. (pause)
We may have to buy her back.

JACE
I can cash in a few things.

HELEN
I have money.

JARED
Are you sure?

HELEN
That's my niece out there! She's
my only family.

Helen turns to Jace.

HELEN
You'll do whatever it takes?
Whatever it takes?

JACE
I'll bring her home.

Helen turns back to Jared.

HELEN
I'm sure.

JARED
Move fast, both of you. Be back
here by ten am.

HELEN
Quicker than that.

Helen leaves in a hurry.

JACE
I need to know who and what I'm
dealing with out there.

JARED
Jace, the only people who know
are dead. And Davey.

JACE
Someone a few blocks away
knows.

JARED
He knows but he's not talking.

JACE
He'll talk to me.

INT:DAY:ATBARAH:WAREHOUSE:EL HAAK'S
OFFICE

Salim has just finished explaining in Arabic.

Davey watches Salim's face closely, not understanding a
word.

Asaad is triumphantly amused. Davey is disgusted and
angry.

DAVEY
How could you? You stood there
and...

Salim cuts her off quickly.

SALIM
(coldly)
I did what had to be done. I do
that.

ASAAD EL HAAK
(laughing)
Back outside, Salim.

Asaad el Haak continues to chuckle to himself.

ASAAD EL HAAK
The Great America. The new land
for the children of the old lands.
Were you born an American, Min.
Thompson?

MIN. THOMPSON
Yes.

ASAAD EL HAAK
Where in America were you
born?

MIN. THOMPSON
El Paso.

ASAAD EL HAAK
A Texan. How about you, Miss-

DAVEY
Dallas.

Davey stares at El Haak coldly.

The GPS barrette still functions in Davey's hair.

> ASAAD EL HAAK
> Two Texans! The cowboy and his cowgirl from the Wild West. JR Ewing. The land of oil and greed. Texas was a slave state prior to America's own Civil War. With great fields of cotton picked by, I believe it was, slaves. Am I right, Min. Thompson?

> MIN. THOMPSON
> That's true, for a brief period.

> ASAAD EL HAAK
> Would it not be a most intriguing irony to learn that your ancestor's once owned, Miss Dallas' ancestors? And now you are here to make amends by teaching Miss Dallas how to set slaves free.

Min. Thompson is silent.

INT:NIGHT:DALLAS:MISSION

> JACE
> Mighty quiet around here all by yourself. I guess you're running the whole show now.

> DENNIS
> I already told the Congressman that I don't know what's going on. I have no idea.

                    JACE
          Not even one idea?

Dennis shakes his head as Jace moves closer.

                    JACE
          No clue, huh? Not the slightest
          idea. Not even a teeny, tiny, little
          speck of an idea.

Jace stalks and circles Dennis around the room.

Dennis is afraid.

                    JACE
          How about a guess? Just, throw
          out your wildest theory. Your
          boss and your co-workers went
          with Davey to free slaves. They're
          dead. She's kidnapped. What
          happened in the middle of that?
          Made any calls? Found out
          anything? Contacted any
          embassies? No?

INT:DAY:ATBARAH:WAREHOUSE:EL HAAK'S
OFFICE

                    ASAAD EL HAAK
          You must feel very at home in the
          Middle East, Min. Thompson. It
          is not so different, I think. Do you
          like it here? You are here.
          Therefore, you must surely like it
          here.

INT:NIGHT:DALLAS:MISSION

Jace backs Dennis into a corner.

          JACE
You know you're about to piss in your
That twinkle in your eye that tells
me you're about to piss in your
pants also tells me you know
something. I wanna know
something too, Dennis.

INT:DAY:ATBARAH:WAREHOUSE:EL HAAK'S OFFICE

          ASAAD EL HAAK
You've already experienced so
much of the joy and pain there is
to find here in the desert. Your
unfortunate pain. My ever-lasting
joy. There is not much else to
know.

INT:NIGHT:DALLAS:MISSION

          DENNIS
It's not my fault!

          JACE
What did you do?

INT:DAY:ATBARAH:WAREHOUSE:EL HAAK'S
OFFICE

          ASAAD EL HAAK
My highest regards to your
Brother Dennis.

Davey stares, horrified at the cruel smirk of Asaad el Haak. A voice from the past zings through her mind.

> DENNIS
> (voice)
> People will steal, kill, and cheat to protect their money. Don't be fooled by hidden agendas.

Davey realizes the betrayal.

Asaad el Haak holds a sword.

Min. Thompson knows he will die.

He looks at Davey who realizes the same.

Davey's eyes well up with tears.

> MIN. THOMPSON
> Davey, don't cry.

Davey looks pleadingly at El Haak.

> DENNIS
> (voice)
> I've got pretty ambitious plans. Don't be fooled... Don't be fooled...

Asaad el Haak decapitates Min. Thompson.

Davey screams.

INT:NIGHT:DALLAS:MISSION

> DENNIS
> They were to be held. That's it!

                    JACE
          Wow. Not so tiny an idea after all.
          Now we're getting somewhere.
          Then what? You'd raise the alarm
          and get additional funding. You'd
          be a hero?

Jace follows Dennis's glance downward to the desk. Jace
snatches up the scratch pad with numbers on it.

                    JACE
          So the hero keeps his eyes on the
          prize. What's this figure?

                    DENNIS
          He wasn't supposed to kill
          anyone.

                    JACE
          He who? You treacherous,
          snakey, son-of-bitch. Who?

Dennis hesitates.

Jace slams Dennis's head against the desk in anger.

Dennis sobs in pain and fear.

INT:DAY:ATBARAH:WAREHOUSE:EL HAAK'S
OFFICE

Asaad el Haak smiles cruelly at Davey's horrified sobs
and the blood spattered on her face.

                    ASAAD EL HAAK
          He will always be part of Sudan.

INT:NIGHT:DALLAS:MISSION

                    DENNIS
          They said they would kill me.

                    JACE
          Ah! Noo. Is that what has you all
          upset, Dennis? Look, it's gonna
          be okay. It's gonna be all right.
          They won't kill you. I'm not
          gonna let them. They won't get
          anywhere near you. You see cause
          (pause) I wanna do it.

Jace sounds like a pleasant television ad from a
pharmaceutical company.

                    JACE
          Are you having difficulty
          breathing? Seeing spots in front
          of your eyes? Is your heart
          pounding? Are your lungs
          bursting? That feeling... that
          feeling, Dennis... is death. Can
          you taste death bubbling up in
          the back of your throat? Kind of
          acid? Kind of acrid and sour? Tell
          me about death, Dennis. Tell me.

Dennis gasps and gags.

                    JACE
          TELL ME! Who?

                    DENNIS
          You can't do this to me.

Jace laughs.

                    JACE
                (laughing)
        You're a Christian, Dennis.
        Believe in miracles.

Jace tightens his grip and shakes Dennis.

                    JACE
        Answer!

                    DENNIS
                (coughing)
        Asaad. Asaad el Haak.

INT:DAY:ATBARAH:WAREHOUSE:EL HAAK'S
OFFICE

The GPS barrette sits close to the henchman's fist balled
tightly in Davey's hair.

El Haak holds the sword aloft then swings chopping off
part of Davey's braids.

Davey screams in fear.

                ASAAD EL HAAK
        Miss *Davey* the Dallas Cowgirl.

He scrapes the sword up and down Davey's neck softly
leaving marks.

Davey shudders and cries from pain, thoroughly
terrorized and broken down.

INT:NIGHT:DALLAS:MISSION

> JACE
> I bet even the Devil hates your
> fake Christian ass.

INT:DAY:ATBARAH:WAREHOUSE:EL HAAK'S
OFFICE

> ASAAD EL HAAK
> My assistants appear extremely
> eager to introduce you to our
> (pause) special ways.

He smiles as Davey is taken back to the room with the
other captives by Henchman #1.

INT:NIGHT:DALLAS:MISSION

> JACE
> Don't you go anywhere, Dennis. If
> you run, I'll find you. And if I
> don't, though I will, a certain
> person you and I both know has
> the resources to find you as well.

EXT:NIGHT:DALLAS:ROAD

Jace calls Jared from his car.

> JACE
> It was Asaad el Haak. Dennis sold
> them all out for a percentage of
> ransom money.

                    JARED
El Haak? Jesus. What that little
asshole fuck didn't know was el
Haak is a psychopath who hates
Christians and Americans about
equally. They never stood a
chance to survive. And now he
has Davey.

                    JACE
We'll get her. I'm closing up shop.
Picking up some gear. I'll be back
at your office in the morning.

Jace hangs up and looks at the empty storefront.

INT:DAY:ATBARAH:WAREHOUSE:SLAVE ROOM

Henchman #1 stands and stares at Davey.

Davey shivers, still in shock, and looks away.

INT:DAY:ATBARAH:WAREHOUSE:EL HAAK'S
OFFICE

Asaad el Haak screams in Arabic.

                ASAAD EL HAAK
Take them away and bury them.
Bury them deep into Sudan.

Henchmen #2 & #3 collect the bodies.

INT:DAY:ATBARAH:WAREHOUSE:SLAVE ROOM

Davey has brief flashback to her childhood watching her mother, MARIAN, being menaced by her father, DAVID.

> DAVID
> Give me the money, Marian!

> MARIAN
> There ain't no more.

> DAVID
> Well, you better find it. Bitch, I'll
> kill you.

> MARIAN
> Please David. Please! You already
> took the last of it. No!David,
> don't! No!

All of the slaves, including Davey, are cowed.

Henchman #1 hits Davey with a gun and speaks Arabic.

> HENCHMAN #1
> Get up filthy black bitch.
> American slut.We are your god
> now!

Davey follows him in a shocked trance.

INT:DAY:ATBARAH:WAREHOUSE:RAPE ROOM

Davey removes her shirt palming the camera with her hand as she removes her bra.

Henchman #1 sets down his gun and pulls his penis out. Davey kicks him hard, then cuts off his scream with a blow to the throat.

Davey has another flashback to the moment when David strangled Marian to death.

Davey strangles Henchman #1. She takes his clothes, knife, gun, and radio.

INT:DAY:ATBARAH:WAREHOUSE:SLAVE ROOM

Davey peeks her head out of the room at the captives sitting facing the wall. They are still unguarded.

> DAVEY
> Ssss.

Davey passes the equipment to the Mother who was raped, but Davey keeps the gun.

Davey holds the gun behind her back. Henchman #2 enters the room and reaches for her. Davey brains Henchman #2 with the gun butt as Henchman #3 enters behind him.

Two of the other women drag Henchman #3 to the floor. Mother uses the knife to slice Henchman #3's throat.

The women kick and knife and spit on the dead bodies.

In the midst of this wordless chaos, Davey strips them of their hardware and parcels it out.

Asaad el Haak walks in and raises the alarm.

Davey shoots but misses him.

Other random slavers shout on their way to the room.

> DAVEY
> Get up and fight them! Fight for
> your lives! Fight!

Davey shoots as many slavers as she can. The other
women begin to shoot. One woman is a great knife-
thrower.

As each man falls, they take his weapons and equipment
until everyone is armed.

> DAVEY
> English! Does anyone speak
> English?

They shake their heads. One BOY raises his hand.

> DAVEY
> What's your name?

> BOY
> Denzo.

> DAVEY
> Denzo. Denzo?

> DENZO
> Like in the movies.

> DAVEY
> I... see. I think. Okay, stay with
> me. Tell them, we're gonna take a
> truck.

DENZO translates. The women nod back at her.

EXT:DAY:ATBARAH:WAREHOUSE

The former captives sneak to the large truck in which they were transported.

Random slavers open fire.

Two women fall. The other women fire back.

> DAVEY
> Everyone get in! Now! Hurry!

Davey lets loose with her automatic and pushes Denzo inside the passenger side of the cab. The other women pile into the back and continue firing.

INT/EXT:DAY:ATBARAH:WAREHOUSE:WOMEN'S TRUCK

Davey pulls YOUNG GIRL and Mother into driver's side.

Davey fires out of both windows.

Then she sees Salim standing with his gun pointed towards them. Salim fires several shots over the hood of the truck.

Davey freezes. They stare at each other a moment.

Salim fires over the truck's hood then points his weapon directly at Davey as an incentive.

Davey breaks eye contact and points to the wheel.

> DAVEY
> Drive!

                    MOTHER
                    (in Dinka)
         I don't know how to drive.

Davey points gun at Mother who screams incoherently.

                    DAVEY
         Dammit, bitch! Drive now!

                    DENZO
         She doesn't know how.

                    DAVEY
         Shit! This means stop. This
         means go. Push go. Push it!
         Get us out of here!

Denzo translates also screaming.

Mother stomps on the accelerator and then the brake,
frightened. The passengers jerk around.

Davey shoots nameless henchmen who try to stop the
truck. She looks back and sees women shooting out of
the rear of the truck.

Mother gets the truck going and they pick up speed.

                    DAVEY
         Faster!

Davey finds shells in the glove box and under the seat.
She loads her weapon.

Davey looks in the back while holding up shells. A
woman nods back at her and holds up more shells.

Davey crawls back and shows other women how to reload then crawls back to the front.

Denzo continues to translate.

> DAVEY
> Where can we go to reach safety?

> MOTHER
> Ethiopia. It is Christian. There are people that will help.

> DAVEY
> How far is it to the border? Do you know the way?

> MOTHER
> I have traveled this road. It is four hours. But it is dangerous.

> DAVEY
> What about the police?

Mother doesn't answer but throws Davey a "you must be kidding" look. Davey checks the gas.

> DAVEY
> Never mind. Full tank. The slavers must have stopped to refill, relax, reload, and rape at the same time.

They are chased by two cars and two trucks.

Davey shoots the engine of one truck which explodes and runs off the road.

She shoots the front tires off a car which turns over and over behind them.

She screams at the women in the back who are shooting out the windows of the other truck and car.

> DAVEY
> Shoot the tires! Shoot the tires!

She screams at Mother.

> DAVEY
> Drive faster!

The women aim for the tires and miss.

Davey looks at the young girl seated on the floor of the truck next to her mother and beside Denzo.

> DAVEY
> What's your name?

Davey has the automatic under the chin of Mother as she shoots out the driver's window.

> YOUNG GIRL
> Beyanzi.

> DAVEY
> Beyanzi? Don't tell me. Not
> Condoleezza Rice or Winnie
> Mandela. Okay… Beyanzi. You're
> gonna have to help me protect
> your mother.

Davey checks outside her own window.

Then Davey hands BEYANZI an automatic weapon.

Beyanzi's mother protests.

                    DAVEY
        Look! The only way you're gonna
        live and she's gonna live is if she
        learns how to kill. I can't cover
        the whole truck and they're
        gunning for *you*.

Davey reaches out the driver's window and shoots
another bad guy.

Mother nods but still looks unhappy about it.

Davey shows Beyanzi how to shoot and reload.

Beyanzi shoots out the driver's window. She aims for the
tires.

EXT:DAY:DALLAS:JACE'S HOME

Beside Jace's sportscar, Jace shakes someone's hands.

                    JACE
        Good deal, man.

INT:DAY:DALLAS:BANK

Helen sits at a desk.

                    BANK OFFICIAL
        Ms. Lewis, are you entirely sure?

                    HELEN
        Is it my money or your money?

BANK OFFICIAL
Your money, of course, but-

HELEN
Is it my house or your house?

BANK OFFICIAL
It's your house, Ms. Lewis.

HELEN
As long as you're clear.

EXT:DAY:DALLAS:JARED'S OFFICE:DOOR

There is a sign on the front door "Office closed today.
Family emergency. Please call tomorrow."

INT:DAY:DALLAS:JARED'S OFFICE:RECEPTION
AREA

Davey's desk has her nameplate, a picture of her and
Helen, and dead flowers from Jace.

INT:DAY:DALLAS:JARED'S OFFICE:PRIVATE OFFICE

Jared is on the phone. He hasn't changed clothes.

JARED
Yes Janell, please call everyone
else to let them know an
emergency has come up and the
office is closed today. Yes, come
in tomorrow. But I will be taking
a few days emergency leave.
Forward all calls to my cell.
Thanks.

Jared hangs up and makes another call.

                    JARED
          I'll call back with the timetable.

                    BIG BUSINESS
          24 hours, Bradley. After that, no
          cover.

An hour and half later, Helen returns as Jace is dropped off.

                    JARED
          She's on the move due east. That
          doesn't make any sense. Unless-

                    HELEN
          Unless what?

                    JARED
          I'm almost afraid to say. She may
          have escaped. That would be near
          impossible. But it would make
          sense. They wouldn't take her
          east.

                    JACE
          I've seen Davey in action.

Helen looks at Davey with eyebrows raised.

                    JACE
          Long ago on the street. She's
          tough. If there were any way to
          escape, she'd find it.

                    HELEN
          She didn't escape you.

                    JACE
          She won't escape me this time
          either. They don't know her like I
          do.

Helen thunks down a sawed-off shotgun engraved with
her initials and a pistol on Jared's desk.

She stares defiantly at the men who look at her in
amused disbelief.

Jared begins to speak but then Helen slams down two
boxes of bullets.

Jace quietly and deliberately puts the weapons and boxes
into a black leather bag.

                    JARED
          Tonight. Two stops to pick up fuel
          and supplies and equipment.
          We'll set you down in Gondor,
          Ethiopia. Cross the border. Find
          her. Bring her back and take off.

                    JACE
          No questions asked or answered.

                    JARED
          Anyone holds their hand out, put
          something in it.

                    JACE
          Clear.

                    JARED
          Jason, son, if anything should
          happen, the US government will
          have to deny...

                    JACE
          ...any knowledge of my existence
          and purpose.

Jared grips Jace. Helen hugs Jace.

                    HELEN
          Stay safe. And please bring my
          baby home.

INT:DUSK:DALLAS:PARKING GARAGE

Jace is met by a dark tinted humvee which transports
him to a private plane.

EXT:DAY:SUDAN:LONELY ROAD

Dust storm kicks up.

Mother backs the truck into the garage of a non-descript
abandoned building.

The dust storm hides the truck's tracks.

                    DAVEY
          Can they travel in this storm?

                    MOTHER
          No. No one can. We're safe for
          the night.

INT:DAY:SUDAN:ABANDONED BUILDING:GARAGE

Two women stand guard at the window next to the
garage.

INT:DAY:SUDAN:ABANDONED
BUILDING:GARAGE:TRUCK

The ex-captives turn on a few handheld lights and find
dried food packets and two jugs of water to ration.

> MOTHER
> What is your name?

> DAVEY
> (sarcastic)
> Oprah Winfrey. No, I'm kidding.
> My name is Davey.

They all laugh at Davey's joke.

> YALI
> I am Yali from Nuer.

> MARY
> I am Mary also from Nuer

> NISA
> I am Aretha Franklin.

They laugh and tell Nisa to sing.

> NISA
> No! I am joking too! I am Nisa
> from Anuak.

> MOTHER
> I am Sara. My daughter is
> sleeping. Her name is Mary, but,
> as you all know, she likes to be
> called Beyanzi.

They smile and finish the role call.

Two of the women, Lati and Robi, are twins.

All the women talk amongst themselves in Dinka and Arabic.

>   DAVEY
> What does your family do for a
> living?

>   SARA
> Our people raise cattle. We have
> done that for as long as we can
> remember. Also sheep and goats.
> They destroyed our village. Killed
> the men. Took the women.
> Nothing left. What does your
> family do?

>   DAVEY
> It's just me and my auntie. She
> takes care of the house and the
> garden and me. She makes
> clothes. I work for a congressman
> in Dallas.

>   SARA
> A congressman? Someone
> important in the American
> government?

>   DAVEY
> Yes.

YALI
If they can capture you and sell
you, then none of us are safe.
Will this congressman come for
you? Will he buy you back?

Davey looks slightly ill.

DAVEY
He told me not to come.

SARA
Then why did you? Why did you
come from America to this?

Davey looks down in deep thought. Then she
looks at Denzo and reluctantly tells her story.

DAVEY
Most African Americans are
descendants of slaves. Slavery is
against the law there now, of
course. But, I (pause) made a lot
of mistakes. I (pause) did things.
Many things, many times. I was
held in jail because I (pause) hurt
people. Took things from them.
For five years, I belonged to the
government. My life wasn't my
own. My name wasn't even my
own.

EXT:DAY:DALLAS:JUVENILE
DETENTION:BASKETBALL COURT:FLASHBACK

Davey is a leader and motivator.

Davey's team wins the game and there is muttered trash talk from ROCHELLE, the largest member of the losing team.

Davey waves Rochelle off.

MARIA slaps Davey 5.

> MARIA
> How many days you got?

> DAVEY
> *Damn* some days. I'm counting down the hours and the minutes. Thirty-six. No. Thirty-eight hours and thirty minutes and I'm out of this fuckin' dump.

> MARIA
> Maintain your composure, girl.

Maria flicks her eyes at Rochelle.

> DAVEY
> Oh, always. You know me.

> MARIA
> Exactly. I know you.

INT:DAY:SUDAN:ABANDONED
BUILDING:GARAGE:TRUCK

Sara looks at Davey in new comprehension.

                    DAVEY
          They assigned me a number and
          that was my name. Then the
          mission offered me an
          opportunity to get out of jail and
          make up for what I did. Make
          the world better. But I will fight
          anyone who tries to lock me up
          again. I'd rather die.

Denzo is tired from translating.Davey gives him a hug
and allows him to sleep against her.

Davey and Sara take their guard shift at the door.
Neither speaks.

Davey stares through the darkened window lost in
thought.

EXT:DAY:DALLAS:JUVENILE
DETENTION:BASKETBALL COURT:FLASHBACK

Rochelle shoves Davey.

Davey goes nuts and beats Rochelle down to within an
inch of her life with a rock and kicks her in the stomach.

Two prison guards yank Davey away from Rochelle.

INT:DARKNESS:DALLAS:JUVENILE
DETENTION:SOLITARY CONFINEMENT:FLASHBACK

Davey sits in the dark rocking back and forth.

INT:DAY:SUDAN:ABANDONED
BUILDING:GARAGE:TRUCK

Sara hugs Davey who cries.

INT:NIGHT:DALLAS:LEWIS HOME:KITCHEN

Jared assembles computers and phone lines.

>   HELEN
> Welfare, foster care, juvie... The
> State of Texas raised her. They
> stepped up to the plate when I
> didn't.

>   JARED
> Helen-

>   HELEN
> No. It's true. I can say it. I wasn't
> there for her when she needed
> me. I love that little girl so much.
> (sighs) I could kill that no-good
> Brother Dennis for what he did.

>   JARED
> I should have parachuted you in
> with Jace.

They laugh.

>   HELEN
> You raised him?

JARED

I had just finished active duty when my older brother, Jason, got killed handling a robbery. I stepped in to help his wife look after my nephew. She never completely recovered from it though. She committed suicide less than a year later. Jace was sixteen.

HELEN

Oh my God.

JARED

He's been chasing my brother's shadow for years. But the reality of a cop's life is kill or be killed. There had been too much death in the family already. I think he picked out Davey on the liquor and convenience store circuit for a reason.

HELEN

Don't remind me.

JARED

Maybe it was revenge. Or a rescue project. Maybe to tell himself that he was okay with his father's death. Then something... well, you know... *something*.

HELEN
(laughing)
I know. Davey has that kind of
effect. She changes people.
Motivates them to do better.

Jared nods thoughtfully.

JARED
So feel good that you're doing
better, Helen.

Helen smiles.

EXT:NIGHT:GONDOR:AIRPORT

Jace's plane touches ground in Gondor and he heads for
a waiting humvee.

Money changes hands with the driver, Salim, who
salutes then leaves the scene.

The PILOT helps him to load his equipment.

PILOT
You are lucky that we missed the
rough part of the dust storm.

Money changes hands again.

INT/EXT:NIGHT:GONDOR:AIRPORT:HUMVEE

Jace checks Davey's GPS from inside the humvee and
guns the motor.

INT:DAWN:SUDAN:ABANDONED
BUILDING:GARAGE

The women plan the last leg of the trip while loading.

> DAVEY
> How much further?

> SARA
> We think, one and a half hours to
> the border.

Davey turns on one of the radios they took from the
henchmen. There is static as she fiddles with it.

> DAVEY
> You know, Denzo, we couldn't
> have come this far without you.

> DENZO
> I am glad to be away from those
> men too.

> DAVEY
> Your English is so good. Why
> didn't you say anything when I
> first spoke into the truck?

> DENZO
> I didn't think my English was
> good. And, I was afraid.

> DAVEY
> How did you learn?

> DENZO
> My parents sent me to a mission
> school in Nasir and I learned
> there.

                    DAVEY
          Your parents-

Denzo looks down sadly.

                    DAVEY
          What happened?

                    DENZO
          Soldiers came. They killed
          everyone except the children. I
          don't know where they took the
          others.

                    DAVEY
          We're going to get out of here.

Davey hugs Denzo and he hugs her back.

                    DAVEY
          I wish that that had never
          happened to you, Denzo. But I am
          so glad that you survived. We owe
          you our lives.

EXT:DAY:SUDAN/ETHIOPIA BORDER:HUMVEE

Jace is stopped by POLICE OFFICER #1.

                    JACE
          Shit!

Police officer #1 approaches Jace's window.

INT:DAY:SUDAN:ABANDONED BUILDING:GARAGE

Denzo has the radio now and turns the knobs. They hear static and rapidly-spoken Arabic.

> DAVEY
> What are they saying?

EXT:DAY:SUDAN/ETHIOPIA BORDER:HUMVEE

Police officer #1 holds out his hand.

INT:DAY:SUDAN:ABANDONED BUILDING:GARAGE

> DENZO
> They are saying. I think they're saying. "There is an old building up ahead has anyone checked?"

> ARABIC VOICE ON
> RADIO
> They couldn't have gone far in the storm. They have to be there.

Denzo screams in Dinka.

> DENZO
> They found us!

EXT:DAY:SUDAN/ETHIOPIA BORDER:HUMVEE

Jace throws money at the Police Officer #1 and roars away in a cloud of dust.

INT:DAY:SUDAN:ABANDONED BUILDING:GARAGE

The women speak in Dinka and pick up weapons.

>DAVEY
>Tell me in English! What did they
>say?

Denzo translates.

>DAVEY
>How many are coming?

Denzo listens again.

>DENZO
>They don't say how many. Some
>from the south. The way we came.
>Others from the north. They are
>meeting here.

>DAVEY
>How far away are they?

EXT:DAY:SUDAN:LONELY ROAD

The trucks roar towards the building from the north and
south stirring dust.

INT:DAY:SUDAN:ABANDONED BUILDING:GARAGE

>DENZO
>I don't know. They don't say.

>DAVEY
>Tell everyone this.

Davey looks at the women as Denzo translates.

>   DAVEY
> We have to protect each other. No
> one will do it for us. We fought
> them yesterday. We will fight
> them today. But we have to move
> fast before they get here. Mary
> and Sofi, both of you guard this
> entrance. Raise the alarm if you
> see anyone.

Mary and Sofi move to guard the door.

>   DAVEY
> Resi, Nisa, Donna, and you four
> find every outside door. Barricade
> them with whatever you can find.
> Hurry! Lati and Robi, load up our
> weapons. Beyanzi, help them
> load. I showed you how. Find
> every bullet. Quick!

Lati, Robi, and Beyanzi start loading the weapons.

>   DAVEY
> Susan, Sara, and Yali, find good
> positions for shooting. We also
> need a hiding place in case we
> need to retreat. Everyone meet
> back at the truck in five minutes.

Susan, Sara, and Yali go off to search.

>   DENZO
> What should I do?

                    DAVEY
          Stay with me. Tell me what they
          say.

Denzo fiddles with the dial of the radio. Davey checks
her weapon. There is a voice on the radio.

INT/EXT:DAY:SUDAN:LONELY ROAD:EL HAAK'S
TRUCK

El Haak speaks into a radio.

                    ASAAD EL HAAK
                    (in English)
          Miss Dallas. Miss Dallas. I know
          that you are still out there playing
          cowgirl from Texas. How
          extremely rude and very shallow
          American of you to leave without
          saying goodbye. And we will not
          discuss stealing my truck and
          killing my men.

INT:DAY:SUDAN:ABANDONED BUILDING:GARAGE

Davey looks disgusted and angry. El Haak shouts.

                    ASAAD EL HAAK
                    (voice)
          Are you listening Miss Dallas
          Cowgirl? We will find you! We
          know you have not reached the
          border. You will never leave
          Sudan. I will cleanse you myself-

Davey is shaken and switches the radio off and takes it
from Denzo. She picks up a smaller automatic gun.

DAVEY
Denzo. Have you ever held a gun?

EXT:DAY:SUDAN:LONELY ROAD:HUMVEE

Jace notices other cars on the road headed the same
direction he is. He falls back slightly.

INT:DAY:SUDAN:ABANDONED
BUILDING:GARAGE:VARIOUS ROOMS

The women pile up desks and other furniture against
three doors.

INT:DAY:SUDAN:ABANDONED BUILDING:GARAGE

Mary and Sofi see dust through the window and raise the
alarm. Everyone runs back to the truck.

DAVEY
Barricade this door too.
Weapons?

LATI
(halting English)
We load all. This is extra.

Lati hands Davey extra ammo. Davey divides the extra
ammo among the women.

DAVEY
Susan and Yali, where do we
shoot?

SUSAN
Six in front. Six here. Six in back.

EXT:DAY:SUDAN:LONELY ROAD:HUMVEE

Jace sees a building in the distance that the trucks surround.

He parks a distance away and cases the scene with binoculars.

INT:DAY:SUDAN:ABANDONED BUILDING:GARAGE

Davey looks through the window. Two trucks park in the rear and two trucks park in the front.

DAVEY
Remember the plan!

INT:DAY:SUDAN:ABANDONED BUILDING:FRONT ENTRANCE

A few henchmen run out and take positions.

INT:DAY:SUDAN:ABANDONED BUILDING:REAR ENTRANCE

Sounds of breaking glass as the women begin to shoot.

INT:DAY:SUDAN:ABANDONED BUILDING:GARAGE

Shots are exchanged between the women.

The henchmen advance.

INT:DAY:SUDAN:ABANDONED BUILDING:LOADING
DOCK

Yali falls wounded at the door. The firepower of the
henchmen overwhelms them. Davey whispers.

> DAVEY
> Send your angels.

Davey calls for retreat.

> DAVEY
> Retreat! Everyone retreat! Follow
> Sara and Susan!

INT:DAY:SUDAN:ABANDONED BUILDING:GARAGE

Davey lets off a few rounds to cover the retreat.

She runs with Denzo to the rear of the building and
shoots out of the rear windows.

> DAVEY
> Is this everyone? Get in! Hurry!

INT:DAY:SUDAN:ABANDONED
BUILDING:BASEMENT

Denzo locks the basement door and then heads with
Davey to the front with Sara who holds the light. Susan
has the other light nearer the middle.

They approach the tunnel entrance and enter.

INT:DAY:SUDAN:ABANDONED BUILDING:TUNNEL

Shuma drags Yali.

> DAVEY
> Lock the door!

LATI locks the tunnel door behind them and brings up the rear with ROBI.

INT:DAY:SUDAN:ABANDONED BUILDING:GARAGE

Bad guys break down barricades and enter the building.

Yali's blood leads bad guys to basement door.

In Arabic.

> HENCHMAN #4
> Here! Break it down!

INT:DAY:SUDAN:ABANDONED
BUILDING:BASEMENT

The henchmen break down basement door. They shoot blindly around the basement.

INT:DAY:SUDAN:ABANDONED BUILDING:TUNNEL

The women hear the sounds of the henchmen shouting and shooting.

The tunnel leads the women near to where Jace has parked the humvee. He assembles a rocket launcher on the roof.

INT/EXT:DAY:SUDAN:ABANDONED
BUILDING:TUNNEL

Davey cannot believe her eyes.

>   DAVEY
>   Jace!

Jace tenses and pulls a gun then realizes it's Davey.

EXT:DAY:SUDAN:ABANDONED BUILDING:TUNNEL
ENTRANCE

Two women behind Davey curse in Dinka and pull guns on Jace.

>   JACE
>   Wait a second! Damn!

Davey waves the women down.

>   DAVEY
>   What are you doing here?

Jace walks to the tunnel exit and looks down stairs.

>   JACE
>   Just wanted to stop by to see how
>   you were doing. Holdin' it down
>   (looks at Davey's guns) southside
>   style, I see. Come on!

Jace helps Davey out of the tunnel.

DAVEY
How many laws are *you*
breaking?

JACE
Probably all of them.

DAVEY
This humvee's too small for all of
us.

INT:DAY:SUDAN:LONELY ROAD:ABANDONED
BUILDING:HUMVEE

The women follow Davey out of the tunnel. Lati and
Robi pause when they hear banging on the tunnel door.

JACE
I didn't know how many. Is Min.
Thompson-

Davey shakes her head then gestures towards the group.

DAVEY
I'm not leaving without them. We
need the truck.

INT:DAY:SUDAN:ABANDONED BUILDING:TUNNEL

The bad guys find the tunnel door and break it down.
Lati and Robi open fire on the bad guys.

JACE
The truck or *a* truck? There's four
trucks over there. Take your pick.

DAVEY
Just like that.

JACE
Don't act like you don't know
how, Davey. We go too far back
for that.

DAVEY
Fine with me. Sara, behind the
wheel. Drive slow. Stay low.
Denzo and Beyanzi get inside.
Help Yali.

JACE
Davey, you know what to do? You
and me center. Two left front
door. Two right front door. Two
behind each second door. Three
in the back.

DAVEY
Denzo, tell them.

DAVEY
Which truck?

JACE
(sarcastic)
Ah... the closest one?

DAVEY
(shrugs)
Then let's do it. Everyone find
your place!

Davey helps Jace set up the shoulder missile launcher.

Jace shoots the building twice. Then he shoots the other truck in front. Henchmen shoot back.

Inside the tunnel, Lati and Robi exchange heavy fire and back up the stairs of the tunnel exit.

Lati is hit but keeps firing.

Davey sweeps with her automatic weapon.The armed caravan moves forward as Sara drives slowly toward the truck they want.

Jace is surprised to see Beyanzi shooting out the driver's window and Denzo shooting out of the passenger window.

Lati and Robi fall together. The bad guys emerge from the tunnel entrance and begin shooting at the caravan.

Davey points and screams.

>   DAVEY
>   Shoot them!

With Davey's help, the women in the rear lay waste to the bad guys from the tunnel.

Just as the caravan reaches the truck, Sara is fatally shot by bad guys running from burning building.

Davey curses and then goes berserk with the automatic.

Jace helps transfer equipment and everyone, including Sara, from the humvee to the henchmen's truck.

                    JACE
          Davey, come on!

Davey continues to shoot. Jace grabs Davey by the back
of her shirt and pulls her into the truck.

                    JACE
          Davey!

INT/EXT:DAY:SUDAN:LONELY ROAD:ESCAPE
TRUCK

Jace drives. He knows the way back to the Ethiopian
border.

Beyanzi screams and cries from the back.

Davey finds the shotgun and loads it. She notes Helen's
initials with surprise.

A few women fire off shots from the back of the truck as
they zoom away.

                    DAVEY
                 (angrily)
          You will never leave the Sudan.

Davey blows up the last two trucks in the rear by
shooting their gas tanks with Helen's shotgun. The
escape truck is not followed.

EXT:DAY:SUDAN:ABANDONED BUILDING

Asaad El Haak speaks on his radio.

INT/EXT:DAY:SUDAN:LONELY ROAD:ESCAPE
TRUCK

Davey looks into the rear and sees Beyanzi crying and
saying the rosary over her mother's body. Davey counts
the women and realizes Lati and Robi didn't make it.

>   JACE
> Davey, are you okay?

>   DAVEY
> I turned that little girl into a
> killer. Her mother didn't want her
> to do it. But I made her kill. I told
> her to protect her mother. And
> now Sara's dead. Shot right in
> front of her. Oh Jace, what did I
> do to her?

Jace holds her hand and drives with the other.

>   DAVEY
> I turned her into me.

Davey is overcome and starts sobbing.

The women stare at her worriedly from the back. One
woman finds a blanket to cover Sara.

>   JACE
> You turned her into a survivor.
> Davey, shh. You did what had to
> be done. You saved many lives.
> You couldn't save everyone, but
> look back there. They're alive.
> Beyanzi's alive. Denzo's alive. We
> have to get them to safety.

Davey wipes her face.

>   JACE
> You did good, Davey. You did real
> good.

Jace cups Davey's chin.

>   JACE
> But Davey, right now, I need you.
> We all need you. You with me?

>   DAVEY
> I'm here. Are you with me?

>   JACE
> It's the only place to be, Davey.

Jace throws Davey a sidelong look.

>   JACE
> The only place.

There is an awkward pause until Jace turns back to focus
on the road and Davey hurriedly checks her gun.

INT:NIGHT:DALLAS:LEWIS HOME:KITCHEN

Jared speaks on a cell phone. A laptop is on the kitchen
table.

>   JARED
> They're going to need your help.

Helen pours coffee for both of them. Jared hangs up.

                    JARED
          Helen, we've got to get going.

                    HELEN
          Get going where?

EXT:NIGHT:DALLAS:PHONE BOOTH IN SLUM

Helen holds her nose and reads from a script in a high-
pitched nasal.

                    HELEN
          -have your cameras rolling.

                    BRITISH VOICE ON
                    PHONE
          How did you acquire this
          information?

Jared hangs up as Helen exhales.

                    JARED
          The voice is someone they don't
          know. They can't trace us to this
          pay phone or the other ones we
          use.

                    HELEN
          One more call, right?

EXT:DAY:SUDAN:ABANDONED BUILDING:HUMVEE

Asaad el Haak hot-wires Jace's abandoned humvee.

EXT/INT:DAY:SUDAN:ABANDONED BUILDING:CAR

Salim listens on cell phone.

INT:NIGHT:DALLAS:SKYSCRAPER W/ OIL
LOGO:OFFICE

Salim's employer stands in front of window looking out
into the night and the lights of the Dallas skyline.

> SALIM'S EMPLOYER
> Wait, Salim.

EXT:DAY:SUDAN:ABANDONED BUILDING:CAR

Salim watches while three henchmen get into humvee
with Asaad el Haak and drive off together.

> SALIM'S EMPLOYER
> (voice)
> Wait.

Salim stares out of the car window expressionless.

EXT/INT:DAY:LONELY ROAD:ESCAPE TRUCK

> DAVEY
> Do we have enough gas?

> JACE
> We just passed through Kassala.
> We're almost at the border. I'm
> not sure.

Jace glances at Davey with a grim expression.

                    JACE
          It's gonna be close.

There is a loud pop. Davey flinches, cocks the shotgun,
and checks the windows for someone shooting.

Jace jerks the wheel and the truck rolls to the side of the
road.

                    DAVEY
          What happened?

                    JACE
          Flat.

                    DAVEY
          There's an extra wheel
          underneath. Help me.

The women stand guard.

Davey jacks. Jace fits the wheel.

Denzo hands him the nuts then joins the other women.

                    JACE
          You never did ask me why I gave
          up my badge.

                    DAVEY
          I just figured it would be one less
          cop to deal with.

                    JACE
          Protecting and serving you is a
          twenty-four hour job, Davey.
          They wouldn't give me overtime.

DAVEY
Ha ha. But you gave up that
badge long before we even
planned this trip.

JACE
My timing's always off when it
comes to you.

DAVEY
True.

Davey looks at Jace squarely.

DAVEY
Speaking of that, why did you
come to me? What are you doing
here, Jace?

JACE
I came for the extreme outdoor
adventure. I mean look at this
place! Plenty of sun. Shoot outs
with armed thugs. You just can't
get that in South Dallas.

Davey looks disappointed.

DAVEY
Never serious.

JACE
We seriously need to get Yali to a
hospital.

The women see dust in the distance and raise the alarm.

Davey lowers the truck with the jack.

> DAVEY
> Jace, hurry!

Davey starts the truck while Jace finishes tightening the nuts. The women pile into the rear.

The truck is already in motion as Jace swings into the passenger side.

The truck picks up speed and Davey sideswipes the humvee full of bad guys twice as it zooms past. Davey's door hangs off the hinge.

Shots are exchanged and glass breaks as Jace and Denzo fire through the windshield into the rear of the humvee. The bad guys return fire.

The humvee slows and the bad guys gun for Davey. One bad guy uses a hook fastened to a cable to yank Davey's door all the way off.

Davey is shot in the shoulder. She screams and curses from pain and anger.

Jace lays across Davey's lap and lets loose a torrent of bullets out of her door. He kills one bad guy and wounds another. Denzo shoots at the humvee.

The humvee speeds up again. Shots are exchanged.

Asaad el Haak sets up a rocket launcher through the sun roof of the humvee.

Jace shoots the wounded henchman and kills him. Then he shoots the driver, the last henchman.

Asaad el Haak has the rocket launcher locked in position. The driverless humvee drifts off the road.

Davey follows the humvee off road. She speeds up and rams the humvee over and over screaming.

> DAVEY
> Gimme five. On the black hand
> side. Down low.

Denzo, Jace, and the women are thrown back and forth.

Asaad el Haak can't hold the rocket launcher steady. He blows himself up.

Jace grabs the wheel and swerves the truck. Davey, the women, and Jace scream. The truck almost tips over on two wheels and then falls back on all four wheels.

Everyone sits stunned a minute.

> DAVEY
> Too slow. You evil motherfucker.

> JACE
> Did you... ever get that driver's
> license?

> DAVEY
> I passed the written.

Jace makes a face.

> JACE
> How's the shoulder?

> DAVEY
> It's nothing. I can still drive.

                    JACE
          Uhm. No. Back on weapons.
          Remember? Your first after
          school job.

The comment cuts Davey but she makes light of it.

                    DAVEY
                     (mutters)
          Before I knew the benefits of
          health insurance.

                    JACE
          Look, I'm sorry. I was out of line
          on that. But still, give me the
          damn keys.

Davey hands Jace the keys and makes a face.

She looks into the back of the truck.

                    DAVEY
          How are you guys back there? Are
          you okay?

The bruised women stare at her for a moment and then
nod back at her.

The engine hisses from the rammings. The truck creaks
because it's falling apart from bullet holes. Jace gives
Davey a significant look.

They hear choppers overhead.

INT/EXT:DAY:LONELY ROAD:SUDAN/ETHIOPIAN
BORDER:TRUCK

The truck rounds a bend in the road. A line of police
point their weapons. Davey clutches the shotgun, then
lowers it. They are out-gunned.

POLICE OFFICER #2 walks up to the window.

> JACE
> Hello, officer. Is there a problem?

Police Officer #2 doesn't speak English.

Police Officer #1 steps up as Police Officer #2 circles the
truck and looks at the women.

> POLICE OFFICER #1
> This is not what you drove.

> JACE
> Yeah, I know. My other car had
> quit on me a few miles back so I
> just caught a lift.

Police Officer #1 studies Davey's wild hair, and gunshot
wound.

Police Officer #2 stares into the back of the truck at the
women who look back at him with hostility, not
speaking. He sees their guns.

Police Officer #2 walks back to the front and whispers in
the ear of Police Officer #1 who is watching Jace.

The gaze of both Police Officers falls down to Davey's
shotgun. Davey stares back, unflinching and unblinking.
There is a tense silence.

European and Arab news helicopters buzz overhead filming the scenario from the Ethiopian side of the border.

Relief agencies on the Ethiopian side of the border look anxious.

Police Officer #1 holds out his hand.

INT:DAWN:DALLAS:LEWIS HOUSE:KITCHEN

Jared watches the confrontation on streaming video from an internet news station he arranged to be in place.

EXT:DAY:LONELY ROAD:SUDAN/ETHIOPIAN BORDER:TRUCK

>   POLICE OFFICER #1
>   Your passport.

>   JACE
>   Of course.

Jace digs out his passport and slowly hands it over. Police Officer #1 evaluates it with cool sarcasm.

>   POLICE OFFICER #1
>   Mr. Bradley, and of course, that is
>   your real name...

Jace looks hurt.

>   POLICE OFFICER #1
>   I recommend that you do not
>   return...

Police Officer #1 holds the passport up.

> POLICE OFFICER #1
> Particularly not without a visa.

> JACE
> Yeah... real bad traffic around
> here during tourist season.

Jace takes the passport back and salutes.

Police Officer #1 glances at Davey again. She holds his gaze a moment and then looks through the window.

The police allow the creaky truck to pass although they still aim their guns.

The truck barely crosses the border when it dies.

European press and aid societies rush to provide them with medical care and to ask questions.

INT:DAWN:DALLAS:LEWIS HOUSE:KITCHEN

Jared and Helen hug each other.

EXT:DAY:LONELY ROAD:SUDAN/ETHIOPIAN BORDER

Jace and Davey sit with Denzo and Beyanzi. They are all wrapped in blankets. Davey's wound, Yali's, and those of the other women are being treated.

Beyanzi cries out as her mother is taken from the truck. Davey holds her close with the good arm.

> DAVEY
> Those policemen saw my gun.

                    JACE
          It's amazing what $3000 and the
          opportunity for fifteen minutes of
          fame will get you these days.

Jace points to the cameras and Police Officer #1 loudly
barking orders.

Davey hugs Beyanzi and Denzo.

News cameras head their way.

                    DAVEY
          Let's get out of here.

INT:NIGHT:PRIVATE PLANE

Davey stares sightlessly out the window. Her arm is in a
sling. Beyanzi sits next to her.

                    MIN. THOMPSON
                     (voice)
          Don't cry, Davey.

Tears stream down as Davey remembers Min.
Thompson.

Denzo sits next to Jace. Denzo draws something on
paper from the hotel room.

Jace picks up a few sketches. One sketch is of a costumed
woman with wild hair holding a gun.

                    JACE
          Davey?

Denzo nods.

                    JACE
          And this is me. And Beyanzi. And
          the other women.

Denzo nods again.

EXT:NIGHT:DALLAS:LOVE FIELD

Helen, Davey, Jared, Jace, Beyanzi, Denzo reunite on the
tarmac.

Jared shakes the hand of someone in a dark suit with
dark sunglasses who walks away.

INT:NIGHT:DALLAS:LEWIS HOME:DAVEY'S
BEDROOM

Helen tucks Davey in like a little girl.

                    HELEN
          I don't know what happened out
          there, Davey.

Helen gestures at Davey's bandaged neck. Davey looks
pained at the reminder and shakes her head not
speaking.

                    HELEN
          Or what all you went through. I
          can't even imagine. I just want to
          let you know that I'm here. I'm
          always Auntie Helen and I'll
          always love you. No matter what.

Tears roll down Davey's face.

DAVEY
My God sent his angels and he
shut the mouths of the lions.

Davey closes her eyes and huddles closer to Helen.

EXT:DAY:DALLAS:LEWIS HOME:GARDEN

The next day, Davey sits expressionless.

She has a brief flash of being locked into the back of the
truck and of her juvenile detention jail cell closing.

INT:NIGHT:DALLAS:CONGRESSMAN BRADLEY'S
OFFICE:JARED'S OFFICE

Jared speaks to BIG BUSINESS.

JARED
I can't believe this shit and I help
make the laws.

BIG BUSINESS
(voice)
You didn't make the window. So
someone goes under the bus. You
decide who it is.

INT:NIGHT:DALLAS:DENNIS'S APARTMENT

Davey knocks on Dennis's door.

DENNIS
Davey! Davey. I'm so glad you got
out okay. I was worried and I told
your aunt-

DAVEY
May I come in?

DENNIS
Of course, of course.

Davey enters. A news station is on television.

DENNIS
Oh my God, your arm! Can I get
you anything?

DAVEY
I'm not here for long.

INT:DAY:DALLAS:CONGRESSMAN BRADLEY'S
OFFICE:JARED'S OFFICE

BIG BUSINESS
(voice)
Her record as a juvenile
delinquent and former gang
member entered the discussion.

INT:NIGHT:DALLAS:DENNIS'S APARTMENT

DENNIS
I've just been trying to straighten
out some paperwork regarding
the mission. It's a complete mess.

DAVEY
Must be hard on you.

Davey glances around surreptitiously and sees a half-packed suitcase on the bed through the open bedroom door.

>   DENNIS
> Don't get me wrong. I know that
> pales in comparison.

>   DAVEY
> So pale that it's invisible. There is
> no comparison.

>   DENNIS
> Davey-

>   DAVEY
> Why did you do it?

INT:DAY:DALLAS:CONGRESSMAN BRADLEY'S OFFICE:JARED'S OFFICE

>   BIG BUSINESS
>   (voice)
> The word 'terrorism' was
> mentioned. There is the matter of
> your own brother, as well.

INT:NIGHT:DALLAS:DENNIS'S APARTMENT

>   DAVEY
> Was there that much hate inside
> you, Dennis?

>   DENNIS
> Davey, you don't understand.

                    DAVEY
          No. *You* don't understand. You
          didn't see the look in his eyes...

                    DENNIS
          Davey, it wasn't like that.

Davey hits him across the face with her good arm as
tears roll down her cheeks.

                    DAVEY
          Shut up! I'll tell you what it was
          like. He knew. Right before he
          (swallows), before they (pause),
          he knew it was you.

                    DENNIS
          Davey, I didn't know. It was all a
          mistake. It wasn't supposed to...
          what they said...

INT:DAY:DALLAS:CONGRESSMAN BRADLEY'S
OFFICE:JARED'S OFFICE

                    BIG BUSINESS
                    (voice)
          I need your permission and also
          your accountability on this.

Jared sighs with disgust.

                    JARED
          I already know how this story
          ends.

INT:NIGHT:DALLAS:DENNIS'S APARTMENT

Davey takes a step closer to Dennis who backs up and sits at his desk.

Davey quickly flicks her eyes past Dennis's head and sees a passport and an airline ticket on the desk.

>   DAVEY
>   You knew they would die. You did
>   the research. You knew what kind
>   of people we were dealing with.

>   DENNIS
>   No!

>   DAVEY
>   Yes! "People will steal, kill, and
>   cheat to protect their money.
>   Don't be fooled by hidden
>   agendas." Right there, Dennis.
>   Right *there*. You told me who you
>   were.

Dennis is silent.

Tears come to Davey's eyes although her voice is cold.

>   DAVEY
>   Those ambitious plans, how do
>   they look to you now?

Davey drops two items on his desk.

DAVEY
They screamed, you know. They
cried. They (gasping sob) begged
to live. Then they lay there dying
while they were robbed and
kicked and spat on.

DENNIS
Davey, please understand.

NEWS REPORTER
The individual names of the
Christian missionary group from
Dallas recently killed in Sudan
are withheld until the next of kin
are alerted...

DAVEY
(sorrowfully)
You knew... as will others.

Dennis looks wild-eyed.

Davey sees something horrible in his face and
backs away from him towards the door.

INT:DAY:DALLAS:CONGRESSMAN BRADLEY'S
OFFICE:JARED'S OFFICE

BIG BUSINESS
(voice)
They located the bodies where
she said they'd be. They'll be
flown back this week. (sigh) I'll
contact immigration. Then we'll
call it even. It's up to you now.

Jared sits stone-faced.

INT:NIGHT:DALLAS:DENNIS'S APARTMENT

Davey exits the apartment leaving the door ajar.

She pauses to take a cleansing breath.

She freezes, sensing something in the darkness of the hallway.

INT:DAY:DALLAS:CONGRESSMAN BRADLEY'S OFFICE:JARED'S OFFICE

>   BIG BUSINESS
>   (voice)
>   There's no turning back at this
>   point. You know this, Jared.

Jared stares at the wall.

>   JARED
>   Keeping *several things in mind*, I
>   can say that I tried.

Jared looks at his speaker phone.

>   JARED
>   You can say the same.

INT:NIGHT:DALLAS:SKYSCRAPER W/ OIL LOGO:OFFICE

Big Business and Salim's Employer are revealed to be the same man. Big Business/Salim's Employer disconnects and dials a number on his cell phone.

INT:NIGHT:DALLAS:DENNIS'S
APARTMENT:HALLWAY

The hallway is dark, ominous, quiet. Too quiet.

INT:NIGHT:DALLAS:DENNIS'S APARTMENT

Dennis sits at his desk with his head in his hands. He
opens a drawer and reaches for a gun, muttering.

> NEWS REPORTER
> While the death of the leader,
> Asaad el Haak, is confirmed,
> there is speculation that certain
> other key members of the group
> fled the country...

A gloved hand pushes the knob of Dennis's door.

INT:NIGHT:DALLAS:DENNIS'S APARTMENT

> NEWS REPORTER
> In related news, Congressman
> Bradley still has not commented
> on the allegations...

A muffled gunshot is heard.

Two photographs of the missionary slaughter, now
bloodied, lie on the desk next to Dennis's eyes.

Dennis groans and whimpers. A gun is in his hand. His
eyes flick upward.

EXT:NIGHT:DALLAS

Moonlight.

A quick view of Helen's eyes through cigarette smoke-filled air as she takes a drag.

A quick view of Jace's eyes as he looks at his watch.

INT:NIGHT:DALLAS:CONGRESSMAN BRADLEY'S OFFICE

A quick view of Jared's eyes, as he snaps off the light.

EXT:NIGHT:DALLAS

A quieter shot is heard.

INT:NIGHT:DALLAS:DENNIS'S APARTMENT BUILDING

Moonlight.

A quick view of Davey's still, unblinking eyes.

EXT:NIGHT:DALLAS:DENNIS'S APARTMENT BUILDING

The front door to Dennis's apartment building opens and shuts into a silent, dark, Dallas night.

INT:DAY:DALLAS:LEWIS HOUSE:KITCHEN

Jared sits stiffly, uncomfortably at a table as if at
interrogation.

> JARED
> He closed out his bank accounts
> and booked a one way flight to
> Mexico. His apartment was
> completely clean.

Jared, Jace, and Helen sit at the table not quite looking
at each other and not speaking.

> JARED
> They'll pick him up if he tries to
> enter the U.S. again.

INT:DAY:DALLAS:JARED'S OFFICE:RECEPTION

Jared shakes the hands of his staff members.

EXT:DAY:DALLAS:JARED'S OFFICE

Jared and Jace carry boxes outside.

> JACE
> Is it hard to walk away after so
> many years?

> JARED
> Those streets don't love me.

INT:DAY:CHICAGO:HARPO STUDIOS

Close-captioned video of a pillaged Sudanese village is
on a screen in the background.

                    OPRAH WINFREY
          Davina, why did you travel so far
          to risk your life?

                    DAVEY
          Being held in bondage kills the
          spirit and the will to fulfill one's
          own destiny. How do you
          calculate the extent of the human
          potential lost to the slave trade? I
          wanted to be part of the solution.

INT:DAY:DALLAS:PRISON:RECREATION ROOM

Rochelle, Maria, and others watch Davey on television
and whoop, then shush each other.

Gigi, doing a bid sits apart and scowls for a second. Then
she looks back at the television thoughtfully.

INT:DAY:CHICAGO:HARPO STUDIOS

                    OPRAH WINFREY
          Jared, there are so many
          perspectives represented in this
          book. It seems as though you
          covered every angle.

                    BEYANZI
                    (VIDEO)
          My name is Beyanzi...

JARED
To understand what slavery is,
what it means, what it does, one
must ask the slave.

DENZO
(VIDEO)
I speak Arabic, Dinka, and
English...

OPRAH WINFREY
The book is dedicated to Min.
Thompson. Why did you decide
to do that?

Jared and Davey look at one another.

DAVEY
Min. Thompson sacrificed his life
to end the trade of slaves in
Sudan. We wanted to recognize
him for that.

YALI
(VIDEO)
Several of us died. But we fought
back.

OPRAH WINFREY
So, Jared, what's next?

JARED
We hope the first-hand accounts
of the slavery experience, on the
lecture circuit, will raise the issue
to a higher level of urgency in
Washington than in the past.

SUSAN
(VIDEO)
There are others still in bondage.

OPRAH WINFREY
Slavery is an intolerable crime
against humanity. No one should
be a slave. All proceeds of Jared
Bradley's book go to pay for the
effort that rescued Davey and the
other former slaves.

DAVEY
(VIDEO)
I was a slave in Sudan.

OPRAH WINFREY
Thank you so much Jared
Bradley, Davina Lewis, and all my
other guests.

An audience member holds a rumpled, yellow *Dallas Morning News* newspaper clipping, dated December 17, 1989 in hand.

NEWSPAPER CLIPPING
-eyewitnesses, an unidentified
black girl, approximately ten or
eleven-years-old, acted as lookout
in the robbery that resulted in the
death of Dallas police officer,
Jason Bradley.

Jace, seated in the audience with Helen, Denzo, and Beyanzi, grinds up the clipping and smiles at Davey.

> BIG BUSINESS/
> SALIM'S EMPLOYER
> (voice)
> Sleep until I wake you.

Brown hands snap shut a cell phone.

The hands light a cigarette then set the same bloodied photographs Davey gave to Dennis on fire with the lighter.

The photographs drop to the ground.

Then a pair of glasses drops on the pile.

Then Dennis's passport, also aflame, drops on top of the pile.

Salim watches the pile burn to a crisp.

> SALIM
> Vaya con Allah, Davey.

Salim grinds the burnt pile into the sand and walks away.

FADE OUT

Acknowledgements

Thank you to all the directors, producers, actors, and screenwriters who persevered to be heard and seen in the face of Hollywood racism, discrimination, exclusion, oppression, and struggle. Despite the overt and subtle attempts to silence the Black voice and ignore the Black presence, you opened doors. Thank you for being seen and heard.

Author's Note

March 2009, the International Criminal Court (ICC) issued a warrant for the arrest of the President of Sudan for war crimes and crimes against humanity related to the civil war in the Darfur region of Sudan. July 2010, the ICC issued a second warrant for the President of Sudan for genocide.

The signing of a Comprehensive Peace Agreement ended the civil war in Sudan, which granted freedom to the southern region of the country. Southern Sudan held a referendum, January 2011.

Southern Sudan seceded and became a free nation, July 2011. I extend best wishes to the people of Sudan in determining the future direction of the nation.

About the Author

Lee McQueen has a B.A. in Political Science and Spanish from Xavier University of Louisiana, a Master of Library Science from State University of New York at Buffalo, and graduate coursework in public policy from the University of Texas at Austin. From time to time, she takes on public affairs assignments—research, data analysis, editorial, copywriting, scriptwriting, fact-checking, proofreading, web content, marketing materials, and social media. Visit the official McQueen Press website at www.mcqueenpress.com for a list of completed projects.

Silk and Silver

I adored you in silk and silver
The words you said
The way they slithered
How I shook
How I shivered
The way you made
Me always quiver
And I always came
Softly back for more
Skin thirsty
I adored
Silk and silver